My First Love

CHERYL BARTON

Published by: CRBarton Productions

For permission requests, write to the publisher, addressed "Attention: Permissions Coordinator," at the address below.

CRBarton Productions, LLC
P.O. Box 962
Reisterstown, Maryland 21136
www.crbarton.com

Ordering Information:
Quantity sales. Special discounts are available on quantity purchases by corporations, associations, and others. For details, contact the publisher at the address above.

Orders by U.S. trade bookstores and wholesalers. Please contact prez@crbarton.com

ISBN: 0-9978779-6-0
ISBN-13: 978-0-9978779-6-0

DEDICATION

Do you remember your first love? Mine was definitely puppy love. I was a young teenager, not yet in high school and I thought that one day I was going to marry him. Unlike other boys, he paid attention to me which is what all young girls wanted. I never forgot who I considered to be my first love. It didn't turn out like Ethan and Valencia's story does in this novel, but I'll never forget it, just as Ethan didn't.

For some people like my parents, that first love was the only love. I love hearing the story of how my parents met when my mom was fifteen years old. For them, it was love at first sight. After fifty-three years of marriage, they are still experiencing, *"their first love"*.

I dedicate Ethan and Valencia's story of finding and holding onto their first love, to all of those who can relate to falling in love and staying in love. I dedicate this love story to my parents, John and Barbara, who have the best love story there is. I love your love!

Happy Reading!

Cheryl

One
Ten Years Ago

"Ethan, who are you taking to the prom?"

"What?" Ethan said. "You ask as if there's anyone else I'd take besides Valencia."

After addressing an absurd question from one of his teammates, Ethan turned back around to his gym locker to continue dressing after another vigorous workout with his friends, all who were a part of the state championship winning basketball team at his preppy private school. Even though the season was over, they still worked out at the end of each school day unless they engaged in a pickup game someplace else. Most days somehow, always consisted of basketball.

"Ah, king Ethan Bennet must be talking about the ever-sexy Valencia Ramos, from the wrong side of the tracks."

Ethan didn't have to turn back around to see the snide look on the face of the last person to make a comment. He knew once the question had been asked, the next flippant comment would come from none other than his team rival and arch enemy, Donnie Anthony. Though they played on the same team and worked as a team when necessary, Ethan would never consider him a close friend. As team captain for the past two years, he knew that Donnie wanted his spot, though he harvested no leadership ability at all. They acted as friends for the benefit of everyone else, but Donnie was always out to get under his skin and making a comment about Valencia was sure to get him the response he was looking for. Thankfully, one of his best friends, Reggie, who knew that any second, he would be pummeling Donnie into the ground, took it upon himself to quickly jump up between the two of them.

A few choice words were in order even while his back was turn, "If I didn't know any better, Donnie, I would say that you're jealous because none of the girls at our school or any other within a million-mile radius would even consider going to the prom with you. Your light as a member of this team isn't even dimly lit enough to make you appealing. I have plans with the ever-sexy Valencia, so I don't have time to entertain you today. Perhaps another day, I'll reintroduce my fist to your face because it's obvious you forgot what happened the last time you said something offhanded to me that didn't sit well. I'll let you have this one since you can't help being jealous of me," Ethan said curtly.

"Guys, let it go. Donnie, you can't insult Ethan when it comes to Valencia. She is beautiful and it doesn't matter where she came from, she's Ethan's girl and we don't touch that; we never hit below the belt on another guy's girl and you know that. Walk away," Reggie said. "Walk away."

As Donnie and a few of the other guys retreated and left the gym, Reggie turned to Ethan.

"Bruh, I saw it in your eyes and if I hadn't been here, you'd probably be looking at a suspension for what I know you would have done to him. You can't get crazy every time somebody makes a comment about Valencia. We all know how you feel about her. Knowing it's a soft spot always gives someone trying to get to you the upper hand."

Ethan knew he shouldn't fall for Donnie's attempts to irritate him, but there were days like today where it was hard to avoid going back at him.

"I hear you. I know it's all about jealousy and you know I've never liked that guy. This prep school is filled with bougie clowns like him," Ethan said, closing his locker and grabbing his bag from the bench, slinging it over his shoulder.

"So, you're going to ask Valencia to your prom tonight? After the party?" Reggie asked as he grabbed his own bag.

Ethan was looking forward to seeing Valencia at the party later in the evening. He had plans for them.

"Yeah, I'm planning on taking her to the ice cream shop we always go to and I'll spring it on her there."

"You really do love her, don't you? I didn't believe it until I saw you turn down girl after girl here at school who were willing to do anything to get with you, but you turn them down one after another day after day."

Ethan looked around and noticed the other guys had left the gym, leaving him and Reggie alone. He felt comfortable talking openly around his best friend, but not the other guys who didn't understand the fact that he didn't want to take advantage of all the girls who threw themselves at all of them, especially him as the star player on the team.

"Reg, we've been friends since ninth grade and you know me better than most people and definitely better than everyone at this school. I have never felt about any girl the way I feel about Valencia. She gets me man, since that first day on the basketball court. There is something special about her that makes her stand out from every other girl I've gone out with and you know there have been plenty of them. This time is different. I know the guys talk about her because of where she's from, but she's better than any of these snooty rich girls here at this school. They aren't better just because they have parents who can afford to pay to send them here and Valencia doesn't. When I say I love her, I mean it and it's not some game."

"I hear you and I can see the difference in your relationship with Valencia than what I've seen when it came to other girls you've gone out with."

That was a fact Ethan knew no one had to tell him.

"That's because there is a difference. She's not just beautiful on the outside man, she's sweet and looks beyond the fact that my family is rich, though I can't get my father to believe that. You know he thinks every girl is out to trap me. Valencia isn't like that. She listens to me and I can talk to her about other things in life that I want to do that may or may not be about basketball. She's the first girl who has ever told me to follow my heart, not the money. That's coming from a girl who has never really had much. You know most girls want to know how much money I'll make one day playing professional basketball. They want me buying them expensive stuff even though they have parents with as much money as mine. Valencia wants me and I want her. She's going to be my future man and that future is going to start with me asking her to the prom after the party tonight."

"I asked Raina last night and she said yes. We should go as couples," Reggie said as they walked toward the exit to the gym.

"Great idea. Let's find out what our ladies want to do and make it happen," Ethan said. He was excited about where the night would take him. He looked forward to the future with Valencia by his side.

Two

Moriah Bennett loved the Miami, Florida heat and today, she had a feeling the ninety-five-degree heat was having a dire effect on her husband's ability to use common sense in his decision making.

"It's for his own good," she heard Tellis say.

She stared in amazement as her husband of over twenty years attempted to defend the rationale behind the poor choice he made when he involved himself in their son's personal life. His nonchalant arrogance was rubbing her the wrong way. "Is it for his own good or for your own good?" she asked, annoyed. "You can't control every aspect of our children's lives, especially Ethan. He loves that girl and nothing you do is ever going to change that."

Moriah knew she was talking to a man who wasn't paying her any attention. After many years of marriage, she could read the signs.

Tellis Bennett was the love of her life, but right now, she didn't recognize the man she fell in love with at a young age, married and raised three children with. He was one of the top players in the national basketball league and a man used to having his way and having people under his control. To him, there was no exception to that when it came to his children. Though she disagreed with his latest actions that could possibly scar their son for life, she knew he loved Ethan and wanted the best for him, but she had a feeling what he'd done wasn't for Ethan's best interest, but for his own.

Ethan was their oldest child at eighteen, Eli their youngest at fourteen and Esha, their beautiful daughter, who at sixteen had recently won Miss Teen Florida. To Moriah, her life was her husband and children and even though they lived a life of luxury as a result of her husband's career, they remained humble, not flaunting their wealth while still living in a manner that showed their appreciation for what they were blessed with.

As Tellis' partner in love and in life, they reminded their children of the importance of an education and being thankful for every opportunity afforded them. She and Tellis were able to provide top-notch education that she hoped would show them that there was more to life than money. She wanted to see them come into their own, making decisions that made them happy in love and in life. Her husband, on the other hand, frustrated her with his need to guide every aspect of their lives, giving their children no freedom in the choices they made. She knew that he had a way of making them think that their decisions were theirs when in fact, he used persuasion to make them see things his way. That worked on Eli and Esha, but not so much on Ethan. With him, Tellis had to find another way to make him see things his father's way. His latest antics, she knew, would be one of the biggest mistakes of his life and she had a feeling they were going to live to regret it.

"Moriah, Ethan has no idea what it means to really be in love. That boy is in lust with a girl over her cute face and body that send his hormones into the stratosphere like every other teenage boy his age. The head he's thinking with could ruin any chance he'll have at a successful career and life," he explained. Tellis was disturbed by the fact that Moriah was fighting him and not going along like she typically did. "That girl will have him locked down with a million kids, leaving him struggling to get by because if he stays with her, they won't be living off of my money. I had her family looked into and her mother can't even keep up with the number of kids she's already popped out and her father is a rolling stone. She doesn't have much of an example when it comes to life's successes and I want more for my son than some young girl who sees the way to success is in between her legs."

Fire brimmed in Moriah as she used her eyes to throw invisible daggers at Tellis. She didn't recognize the man she loved and married. She'd seen him angry over the years, but the words coming out of his mouth were vile and hateful. She did agree that Ethan and Valencia were a little too close for her comfort at their age, but talking down to a young girl they still didn't know a lot about wasn't the answer. Who her parents are didn't provide evidence that she'd be the same way. She preferred talking to their son to be sure he wasn't on the path to make a mistake that could cost him more than he could imagine. If by chance Ethan and Valencia were having sex at their age, she knew that Tellis had talked to him and Eli about responsibility and safety when it came to sexual activity and she knew Ethan wouldn't make a mistake like that. She didn't want to know what her son did in his private time, she only wanted him to be happy, not take risks and be respectful of any girl he decided to get involved with. She wanted all of her kids to find happy, loving relationships like she had with Tellis. What she didn't want was for her husband to lay the ground work for deceit in the name of looking out for their best interests. What he was doing to Ethan was wrong and the choices he made, right or wrong, always came down to money; his money, as he often put it. She was tired of hearing those two words.

Holding back as much of her anger as she could, she addressed his money talk once and for all. "Your money? You think you made that money and achieved success by yourself because you were on the court?"

"Honey, that's not what I'm saying," Tellis said, trying to explain.

Moriah gladly cut him off with her hand.

"You had your say, now I'm having mine," she said with anguish. "What about me and the rest of your family who have supported you from day one? What about all of the times our kids longed for more time with you, but they sacrificed just as I did knowing how much your career and taking care of us meant to you. I love you for everything you've done, achieved and made of yourself, but I love you most for who you are - a man I fell in love with around the same age as our son is right now. You found love and he should be able to do the same on his own terms. We've raised him right and we have to respect who he decides to fall in love with and when and I hope that's the last time you open your mouth and proclaim your money to me," she said harshly.

When Tellis came closer to her as they stood arguing in the living room of their eight-million-dollar mansion, Moriah knew that she'd struck a nerve with him and he'd realize he'd gone too far.

"Whoa, I'm sorry. That was a poor choice of words and I didn't mean it the way it sounded. I am because of you and how you held our lives in check all those years and I love and respect you for that." Tellis hoped his words were ringing true even though he could feel the tension in the room and no weapon, no matter how sharp, could cut through it right now. He needed to choose his words carefully. "When we fell in love, I had nothing and we achieved everything together. I would never, ever discount your role in the life we've built as husband and wife. I am, because we are. You have been my rock, my love, my support and my best friend since I was a teenager."

Moriah paced across the cream Persian rug in the center of the floor and tried her best to contain her anger at him.

"Then I don't understand why you can't see the same love between Ethan and Valencia."

Moriah stared as Tellis joined her in pacing around the room. They haven't had an argument like this in years and this latest quandary was one of his worst. Trying to rap her mind around the repercussions of his actions, she walked over to the fresh flowers she had been arranging when he walked in and told her what he'd done, interrupting her peaceful morning. The yellow and white arrangements strategically placed around the room brought out the gold, beige and cream color scheme of the room. For a split second, her anger had her thinking of picking up one of the crystal vases and tossing it at him to relieve the stress the conversation was causing. She would not give in to him on this and she would not placate him by making him think she was being the dutiful wife and following his lead. She stood her ground even when he walked over to her with his begging face and pleading eyes.

"Honey, she's not the one for him and you know it as much as I do, though you refuse to admit it because you want him to be happy. I do too, but that doesn't mean his happiness lies with the first pair of huge tits and big round behind that comes his way."

Moriah turned in slow-motion like characters do in a scary movie, tilted her head and looked at him sideways.

"So, you're looking at her body parts?" she asked.

Hearing that 'no joking' sound in her voice, Tellis took a step back. They have never been physical with each other, but he had a feeling his last foolish comment could cause her to slap him and reign back in his common sense. He was still putting his foot in his mouth. She was already angry for what he'd done and adding to that, what he'd just said, could cause a fight. He laughed it off to show her there was no need for her anger to boil over as he raised his hands in surrender.

"Don't go there – you know better and you know what I'm saying. The only thing Ethan sees is beauty, but he misses the fact that she has nothing else going for herself. Her family barely scrapes by. This girl lives in a tiny, rundown house with seven other people, a house I understand often has no electricity because they can barely pay their bills. You don't think she sees her ticket out of that through Ethan? Her mother works a just above minimum wage job and what I was able to find out about her father is that he doesn't even have a job. Even if they don't spot Ethan's potential, they know who he is and who we are and I assure you, that girl is being pushed to trap him by any means necessary. I won't have that for my son. He's taking a risk every time he lays up with that girl."

"You don't know that they're doing that."

This time Tellis looked at her sideways. "Trust me, I

know and I also know that's a part of our son's life you don't want to hear about, but I'm on top of it. There will be no little Bennett's running around calling our teenage son daddy," he snorted.

Moriah didn't want to know about her son's escapades and moved beyond that discussion. She decided to let Tellis deal with their sons when it came to that.

"You've met her a handful of times and not once have you ever taken the time to get to know anything about her. You dismiss her and have never been shy about the fact that you don't want Ethan with her. I at least try to support his choice of a girlfriend by being cordial. Now, you're playing a dangerous game. I've always stayed back and let you deal with the boys while I focused on this modeling career that Esha wants to have. When you weren't on the road, I loved the time you spent with the boys, but now Ethan has the chance to make decisions regarding his own life and I've begged you to let him do it. You've pushed back on that and I've relented, now regretting my decision to do so. How could you play Russian roulette with our son's life?"

"I'm not playing anything. What I am doing is making sure that Ethan makes the right decisions when it comes to his life and career. Ever since he was a little boy, he has wanted nothing but the chance to play professional basketball. I've done everything to help him get there including being his personal coach through the years, getting him on the best local teams, encouraging his talent and letting him know that the world was his, and it is. This young girl can ruin everything for him and you're willing to sit back and let him ruin his future for a piece of..."

Moriah turned around so fast, she almost gave herself a whiplash.

"Don't you dare say that next word, not in this house. You know how I am about that kind of language directed at any woman, whether you respect their character or not," she said angrily.

Tellis caught himself and immediately apologized. He never disrespected a woman and even in anger, he knows he shouldn't and never in the face of the woman he loved.

"I'm sorry, baby. I was spouting in anger and I didn't mean anything by it. I would never, ever do that," he implored.

"I'm sorry to interrupt, but Mr. Bennett, you have a call, sir."

Moriah and Tellis looked over at Sarah, a woman who had been with them for years taking care of their household, as she entered the room. Tellis looked at her looking for any sign that she'd be angry if they continued the discussion later.

Moriah waved him off. She could use a break from their argument. "Go ahead and take it. It will give me a few minutes to tamper my anger down a few notches."

To calm her nerves after Tellis walked out, she walked over to the nearest chair and sat down, still fuming and wondering how they were going to get beyond this.

Three

"Hey, mom!"

Moriah looked up and as soon as she saw Esha, she plastered a smile on her face to hide her morose feelings.

"Esha, when did you get home?" She hoped she hadn't heard any part of the discussion with Tellis. "I didn't hear you come in."

"I just walked in through the garage door. Ms. Tyrell brought me home to get my tennis racquet. Laila and I are going to play tennis at their house. Are you okay if I miss dinner? Ms. Tyrell said she was going to feed us before she brings me home later if that's okay with you."

"Is your homework finished?"

"Yes, I did it in the library after school. I'll leave it on the table if you want to check it over. I want you to read over my report and let me know if it sounds good to you. Are you okay? You look funny like you're upset, but don't want me to know you're upset," Esha said.

Moriah tried harder to hide her true feelings.

"I'm fine. What do you think of the new flowers? I was just finishing arranging them after they were delivered today."

"They look nice. We have tons of rooms, but this one is still your favorite, huh?"

Moriah looked around knowing Esha was right; it was her favorite room in the house. The large bay windows that overlooked the massive greenery that surrounded the house was her favorite place to sit and relax. "Yes, it's still my favorite."

"Hey, Esha!" Tellis said entering the room.

Moriah smiled when Esha embraced him. The love between father and daughter has always been evident.

"Hey, daddy. I'm on my way to play some tennis and mom said I could skip dinner."

"That means your mother and I will be eating dinner alone tonight. Ethan is going to some party with his friends and Eli is going out with his team for ice cream after practice."

Esha smiled. "That means you get an evening alone without us. I'm sure you'll enjoy that. My only request is that Eli be the last of your children, so no funny business. I don't think I can handle any more siblings," she joked.

"Esha!" Moriah shouted and laughed. "You better get going before I change my mind," she said.

"Just trying to make you smile. You said you were

okay, but I can tell when something is bothering you. I hope daddy can cheer you up while I'm gone. I'll call you when I'm on my way home. Love you!"

"Love you, too," Moriah shouted at Esha as she ran toward the garage. As soon as she was gone, the fake smile she had plastered on her face for her daughter's benefit disappeared as her attention turned back to Tellis.

"Can we talk with sensible heads now?" he asked before she could speak up first.

"Well, I don't know. I'd like to hear the full story of what you did and I'm thinking by the end of the conversation, you'll be eating dinner alone tonight. Enlighten me on this note that will break my son's heart."

"I didn't do it for him to have a broken heart – I did it so that he could have a bright future."

"Don't sugarcoat what you did. So, what now? Ethan will see this note from Valencia and you think he won't go after her? He's to believe she wrote him some 'Dear John' letter confessing that she's been seeing someone else this whole time and you really think Ethan will believe that? They spend all of their time together. He loves her and won't give up that easily. He's strong-willed just like you and I are and he won't let that go."

"Oh, he'll let it go because it's not just the letter that I told you about; there's more."

Tellis shuffled from one foot to the other knowing that now was the time for him to tell her the complete story behind what he'd done.

"What else did you do?" Moriah asked through clinched teeth.

"Well."

Tellis looked at her and then down at the floor and finally back up at her. Now, when he thought hard about what he'd done, he was ashamed that he would stoop as low as he did.

"Well, what? What else did you do to ruin my son's heart?" As Tellis exhaled loudly, she knew what he was going to say had to be big. "Tell me now, Tellis!" she demanded.

He didn't look directly at her as he spoke. Instead, he glanced out of one of the room's bay windows.

"Her father took the money," he mumbled.

As soon as she heard the word money, she knew it couldn't be good. He thought anything and everyone could be bought with money and she had a feeling, he'd found his latest Guinea pig.

"Money? What money? Tell me you didn't?" she said, looking at him now with disgust. "You did something that involved money changing hands? Are you out of your mind!" she screamed, happy Esha had left.

"Before you pull out any weapons, try to keep calm and let me explain. I had someone offer Valencia's father some money to keep his daughter away from Ethan." Now that he spoke the words out loud, hearing it sounded worse than actually doing it.

Rage was all Moriah could muster up as she tried to focus on the fact that he used money to ruin their son's love life. She could admit that she wasn't sure Valencia had the same dreams and goals as Ethan, but that wasn't for her or Tellis to judge. Ethan not only wanted to play professional basketball, but he wanted post high school degrees and to make a life of his own, not just live off of the life his father provided. According to Ethan, that life was going to include Valencia; that was until Tellis butted in. Though the family had lots of money, Ethan wanted his own and she admired that. How could Tellis play with their son's life like this, she thought?

With the millions on top of millions that Tellis acquired playing ball, he'd turned that into several successful businesses including one of the most popular restaurant chains across the country and his own basketball shoe line that mirrored the Michael Jordan Nike shoe line. He and his brother, Walt, owned a sports management company that managed the careers of the top five players in the country in basketball, football and baseball.

Besides the money he brought in, Moriah was proud of her own career that helped finance the life her family lived. Though Tellis provided well for them, she loved that she also had her own career managing Esha's career as well as several others that she'd recently taken on. With the interest in her management skills, she would soon launch her own talent agency to help launch careers of others who were interested in modeling and other fields in the entertainment industry. She and Tellis loved and lived together, but outside of that, they had their own goals and careers and when she'd met him, she had no idea what she wanted to do in life – still she found her way. She couldn't discount that Valencia would do the same and she was revolted by the fact that her husband felt the need to make their lives what he wanted them to be. She stood, unable to contain her anger while sitting. She needed to move about to keep from screaming at the top of her lungs.

"Money, Tellis? You really got that desperate that you felt you had to pay someone to again extend your control over your son's life? Shame on you. What if Ethan finds out? He will never forgive you. He will never forgive me either for not stopping this mess when I had the chance."

"Our son loves us and nothing could ever make him hate us or get to a point where he wouldn't forgive us, not when he realizes I did everything for him. I would do it for Eli and for Esha, too. With the wealth we have, I have to take great care in who our kids are exposed to and who they let in."

"Do you plan on picking the perfect woman for Ethan that you feel he should fall in love with? What does her criteria have to be? What about Eli and Esha? Do you plan to control who they fall in love with, too?"

"Oh, I already have a game plan in place for the perfect guy for Esha. Luckily, right now she's all about pageants and modeling, but trust me, she won't be bringing home just any old dude talking about she's in love," he said matter-of-factly.

"I don't know where you get this from. You were able to make your own decisions in life and you turned out just fine, but you believe that your own kids haven't been raised in a way that they would know how to make good choices? Are you saying I've been a bad mother? Do you think I didn't instilled in them the values and morals they would need to succeed in life? Not that you haven't had an impact, but we both know they've spent most of their time with me. It wasn't until you retired from the game that they were able to benefit from time with you. I'm not at all trying to slight your impact on their lives, but I don't like what you're trying to insinuate about their upbringing."

Tellis knew he'd said a few words too many and he needed to pull back.

"Okay, I get it, you're mad at me, but don't be mad thinking I don't think you've been a wonderful mother. I'm sorry if that's how you think I feel. Our kids are the great people they are because of you and you kept this house running when I spent month after month on the road. Without you making the sacrifices you did, I wouldn't have been able to have the career I had or the life I have or none of this. I would never speak ill of your care for our children and you know that. I'm saying that because I want to, not because I have to. You know my love for you and them is unconditional and it always will be. That doesn't mean I don't want to help guide them in the right direction. Valencia may be a nice person, but my son needs a woman like you if he's going to make it and I don't think that's her; that's all I'm saying. Ethan is on the path to greatness and he'll need a great woman. I can't apologize for not believing that woman will be Valencia."

"Tellis, you paid someone to interfere in our son's life and that's wrong," she cried.

"No, I paid someone to interfere in Valencia's life; there's a difference."

"Don't try and double talk me. I'm not some business deal you're trying to secure and I'm telling you that you're going to regret invading in his life. If I had known the extent of your deceit, I would not have allowed this, but it sounds like it's too late. I can only hope that Ethan dives into his first year of college and that this won't hurt as much as I think it will."

"Baby, Ethan will be fine and trust me, you'll see that this was the best thing for him. His signing day is in two days and by then, I think he will have moved past Valencia and refocused on school and what will one day be a successful professional basketball career. I know you don't agree with my tactic, but it was for the best. Girls will come and go in Ethan's life. This isn't a time for him to be locked down with some ball and chain to some girl right when he's headed for stardom."

"What if someone had thought the same way about me back when we started dating? You were headed to the draft early and I didn't come from much? Did it feel like I was a ball and chain back then?"

Moriah held up her hand as he was about to reply.

"Moriah, don't," was all he could get out.

"How much?" she asked.

"What?"

"How much was ruining my son's first love worth? How much did it take to buy her father off, a man who barely had a hand in her upbringing, yet he's willing to tear her life down for money?"

Tellis could barely look at her, turning his attention away in shame.

"That's not important," he said quietly.

"Don't look away from me. This is my son we're talking about and everything about him is important. How much?" she shouted, thankful that no one was home to hear her raise her voice at him other than the staff and they've heard them argue before.

"One hundred grand."

"That's all? You're worth over three hundred million dollars and he was okay accepting a measly one hundred thousand dollars?"

"Yeah, well, he was okay taking less, but I sweetened it to be sure he held up his end of the bargain."

"Tell me, what does he plan to do to keep her away? I believe she loves Ethan, so I suspect he won't be able to just put some money in her hands."

Tellis knew the extent that her good-for-nothing father would go to. He refused to tell Moriah that Valencia's father paid someone for uncompromising pictures of Valencia with another boy, knowing that would surely make Ethan walk away from her. The thought made him sick to his stomach. He had no idea the length her father would go to for one hundred thousand dollars, but it was too late now; the damage was already done. He knew that right about now, Ethan was reading the note supposedly written by Valencia which was accompanied by photos that were being shown to him by a friend. It was already done and there was no turning back. Ethan will be leaving for college soon after his televised signing to play basketball for the number one college in the country. There were those who wanted Ethan to go straight to the professional league, but he wouldn't hear of it. His sons, Ethan with basketball and Eli with baseball would be more than just ball players.

"It's done Moriah and there's no turning back. Let's get Ethan through this signing and off to school and in the long run, we'll see that all of this was worth it. Valencia was going to be a distraction and one day, he'll meet an incredible girl, one as wonderful as you are, who can be everything he wants and needs."

As far as she was concerned, the conversation was over. Deep down, she knew that she should fight harder to protect Ethan from the wrath her husband was bringing down on his love life, but she didn't know how to stop what had already happened and at this point, she didn't want Ethan's hate of his father over the situation to ruin his college life and where his life would go in the future. She was done talking about it; what was done, was done.

"I'm going to go out for a while and forget that I'm party to you ruining our son's life."

"You're not a party to any of this. This is all my doing," Tellis said.

She turned to him before walking away.

"We're partners, Tellis. I'm a party to this because I didn't stop you in the beginning when I knew what you were planning to do. Don't ask me to not be upset about this and if my son ends up in a miserable marriage one day, completely unhappy with his life, I will blame you and I will never, ever forgive you for that. Enjoy eating dinner alone tonight. I'm going to the club."

Moriah walk out of the room, grabbed her car keys from the kitchen counter where she'd left them and walked out of the house to her car.

"Baby, wait."

She looked up to see that Tellis had followed her out.

"Not now, Tellis; not now," she said and waved him off as she got in her car, opened the garage door and drove off. As she drove, she prayed that her son would be able to get over the hurt that was about to come down on him.

Four
Four Years Later

The celebration was huge! The crowd in the room cheered as Ethan Bennett took to the stage donning the hat of the professional basketball team that selected him as the first pick in the draft. Everyone suspected he would go first after leading his college team to four straight years of college basketball championships.

At six-foot, seven inches tall, Ethan was a powerful power forward, his game mirrored some of the best who ever played the game including his father who couldn't be happier or prouder of his accomplishments. His father was and always would be his number one hero, but he proclaimed other major influences in the form of Kobe Bryant, Michael Jordan, LeBron James and Scottie Pippen. He considers them, as well as many others, the greatest of all times for their talent on the court. In their own way, they each inspired his acumen as an athlete.

As a college freshman, he averaged twenty-seven points and nine rebounds per game. By his senior year, he was averaging thirty points a game, eight point one rebounds, five point nine assists and four point two steals. Not only did he excel at sports, he also graduated with the highest honors only weeks ago and as the first-round draft pick, he was signing a multi-million-dollar deal with his number one choice of teams in the country.

Following the ceremony, he and his father, who was also his manager, were heading to another signing of a multi-million-dollar endorsement deal with a soft drink company and a with a company that reached out to him to partner in a deal to sell and promote his signature line of hats. Ethan Bennett was known for wearing hats and the public liked what he liked. His head gear line, *E-Ben*, will make him more millions upon millions and thanks to the sports management company that his father and uncle owned, his career would be managed well.

Standing on the podium next to him was his father and Ethan spotted him looking out over the room full of other potential draft picks, families and friends and smiled. This day was well worth the hard work and he loved how proud his father was of not only him, but of his brother and sister as well.

His brother Eli who was the youngest, was sure to be a major player in professional baseball and his sister, Esha, was well on her way to being one of the most successful models to ever grace the stage. One thing

Ethan knew was that his father took great pride in the role he played in helping his kids achieve their goals.

Looking to his left, he saw his mother, Moriah, the best and most supportive mother any child could ask for. Eli and Esha stood alongside her as cameras flashed and people screamed his name. He was about to have everything he'd been dreaming about and it was because of the love, support and dedication of his family.

"Ethan, Ethan! A few words!" someone from the press screamed.

"Well, I'd like to give thanks to my family and friends for helping me get to this day. It wasn't just the hard work, but it was with their love and support that I'm standing here today. I'm grateful that the greatest team to ever play the game of basketball selected me as the number one draft pick today and I won't let them down. I'm looking forward to playing on the team and learning from current players what it means to be a part of this franchise."

Ethan listened as question after question came at him and he tried his best to answer each one of them before his father interrupted.

"Okay folks, there is more to the draft and we don't want to take anything away from anyone else. Ethan will be answering all of your questions as soon as the draft is over. Thank you for your support."

Following his father's lead, Ethan exited the stage and into a secluded room where more family and friends were gathered. He smiled as he was pulled into one hug after another from one family member to another, to one friend to another. This was the best day of his life and he knew that this was just the beginning.

At twenty-two, he was living a life that some only dreamed about and he was humbled by the thought. He was happy knowing the success in life he was achieving, but he also knew that money wasn't everything. It bought a lot of things, but not real, true happiness. He'd had money all of his life because of his father's success and though it provided him with a great life, he knew there was more to it than fame and fortune.

Needing a moment to himself beyond the drinking and celebrating in the room, he excused himself and exited to a room his father had secured for him to get a little privacy. Leaving the celebration, he entered a single hallway with one door to the right, a private room. Once inside, he closed the door behind him and sat down in front of a large big screened television and turned on the rest of the draft. Though his portion was over, he wanted to watch and support the others. Sitting back to focus, he turned when the door to the room opened and his father walked in.

"Ethan? What gives? Everyone is asking for you. This is a day about you. I got you this room for later when you wanted to chill before heading to the hotel," Tellis said.

"Yeah, Pops, I wanted to watch the rest of the draft. There will be plenty of time to celebrate after this."

"You're right. Your mother has organized the biggest celebration known to man for later tonight. This has been some day already, huh?" Tellis asked, sitting down next to him.

"Yeah, it's been an overwhelming day especially after graduation just a few days ago. I've definitely been on a rollercoaster ride."

"That you have been. Where's Talia? I thought she'd be right by your side taking a break from studying for the bar exam. She's going to be one hell of a lawyer and I'm hoping she'll come work for the management company, representing some of the players. Her father's law firm is the best in the country and he's been my lawyer since I played the game many years ago. Introducing the two of you was one of the best decisions her father and I ever made. Isn't she perfect? She's beautiful, smart and will make an incredible wife and mother. It's been three years of dating. Are you planning on making things a little more permanent between the two of you?"

Here he goes, Ethan thought.

"Pop, don't start," he said frustrated. He loved his father, but he had a habit of trying to control everything and Ethan no longer appreciated it now that he was an adult. When it came to his love life, he didn't want anyone's input.

"Start what?" Tellis said, taken back by Ethan's pushback.

Ethan looked over as Tellis relaxed back on the chair, signaling he wasn't going to give him the solitude he came to the room seeking. He needed a break.

"Stop trying to slide a ring on Talia's finger. If or

when I decide to do that, you and mom will be the first to know. Talia is a great woman and she's on her way here. Her flight was delayed unexpectedly due to a case she was researching for her father's firm."

"She didn't think it was important to be here, by your side on time for the draft? This is the biggest day of your life. I'll call her father to see what the delay was that he couldn't get someone else to take that task from her, making sure she was here."

Ethan stopped his father when he reached for his cell phone.

"Let it go – she'll be here when she gets here."

"You're right. You'll have the rest of your lives to fight about her commitment to you. I'm telling you, she'll be the perfect mate coming from the life of being raised by two very successful lawyers. She went to the best schools, graduated at the top of her class like you and now, expected to pass the bar on the first go-round. Nothing beats beauty and brains."

Something does, Ethan thought. His father was right that Talia had beauty and brains and she was going to be a force to be reckoned with in the courtroom, but there were two important things missing in their relationship and they were passion and love. He cared about her and had enjoyed their last few years together, but he wasn't sure she was who he wanted to marry and wake up to for the rest of his life. That thought made him think of Valencia, the one person he has never been able to forget about. One day she was there and the next, he discovered she didn't really love him the way that he loved her.

"Hey, can you give me a minute to myself? I'll come back and join everyone in a few minutes. I'm sure they're wondering where we both disappeared to and any minute, this room will be swamped with people, including mom and she'll drag us both out of here. Give me a minute? You know what it's like at this moment to need a few minutes of peace. You've been here, so I know you understand," he said using the same words of persuasion he'd seen his father use many times.

"I understand and I'll keep them at bay."

Tellis stood to leave and turned back as Ethan looked up at him.

"Pop?" he questioned.

"Ethan, I want you to know how proud of you I am and I love you. Everything I've done is because of how much I love you and want nothing but the best for you."

"I know, Pop; I know."

After Tellis left, Ethan turned the television off and thought back to a time that was a lot simpler than the one he was living today and to a love that was as real as each given day. Even now, he still could not imagine what went wrong.

He and Valencia Ramos had met early in his senior year of high school over four years ago. They were eighteen and from two different worlds. Unbeknownst to his parents, he loved going outside of his pristine, high society neighborhood to join in on pickup basketball games in neighborhoods that his father would bar him from if he knew about his trips there. It was during one of those pickup games that he'd met Valencia, the prettiest girl he'd ever seen. The moment he saw her, he couldn't stop looking at her. Half Puerto Rican and half African-American, she had long dark hair that she let flow down around her shoulders. He still remembered the white shorts and pink and white top she had on. She had curves for days, but it was her smile that drew him in. Every boy was interested in her, but from the start, she only had eyes for him and he for her.

She and some of her friends were watching him and some other guys play ball and he winked at her. When she smiled and winked back, he laughed and fell in love.

After that first meeting, they met up often for burgers and milkshakes whenever he could get away to her part of town, which was made easier one month after they met when his father bought him his first car for Christmas. From that day forward, he would leave his community, pick Valencia up for dates and they hung out whenever he had free time.

He'd fallen in love fast and couldn't imagine not being with her. The first time they'd had sex was in that same car and after that, they had gotten creative with where they did it, not wanting others in their business.

A few times, he'd snuck her into his house when his parents were out or busy doing something else in another part of their large home. He was thankful for Eli, who would be his lookout to keep the house staff away from his room and alert him when their parents came home.

One day his father caught him with Valencia in a compromising position and from that day forward, there was tension. He'd had to sit through an hour-long speech about protection during sex and girls who would be out to trap him. The conversation didn't go well when he became furious at his father who insinuated the kind of girl he thought Valencia was, only dating him because they were rich and that all she wanted was to get pregnant by him like any other girl would do who saw dollar signs. Even though he promised his father he and Valencia always used protection, to him it wasn't enough when he shared stories of women who got pregnant when guys thought they had used the best protection, only to find that those women had schemed and planned. Ethan knew Valencia wasn't like that and he tried to get his father to understand that to no avail.

Once his parents found out about her, he tried to bring her around so that they could see that she wasn't anything like his father thought, but he knew they only placated him with their kindness towards her. Valencia was blind to their true feelings and as long as he could continue seeing her, he let her stay in the dark about his father's true feelings about her. He hated seeing her trying hard to prove she was good enough for him knowing that his father, in particular, never saw any good in her. All he saw was a girl looking for a come-up.

At the end of his senior year, he'd planned on asking

Valencia to his prom and to be his date at his graduation party. He had been excited all day knowing that he'd see her later in the evening at a party some friends were having. She and her girlfriends were having a weekend sleepover and would be arriving together. After the party, they were planning to hang out where he would then ask her in a flamboyant and lavish way that his friends helped him cook up, to be his prom date. Instead, he was greeted later that night with a letter she'd written, her version of a 'Dear John' letter and one of his friends presented him with photos of her hugging and kissing another guy. Totally shocking him, from the look of things, they were about to do more than kiss. He was infuriated and didn't know how things had gone wrong for them. That was a day that still lived with him even today, the happiest day of his life.

The night that she broke up with him by way of a letter, his world had changed and his father's words rang true. Valencia wasn't in love with him like she had declared over and over again. She couldn't be if what he saw on the pictures were true. Everything about that night had continued to live with him. His first instinct had been to find Valencia and have her explain her actions, but he didn't. He held his head up like a Bennett man should do and rather than allow her to continue to embarrass him with her lies and deceit, he moved on from her. He picked a girl from his school to take to the prom and they dated for the rest of the summer until he went away to college. He never went back to Valencia's neighborhood to play ball and he never heard from her again.

Ethan forgot about the draft on the television and only thought about Valencia who should have been with him today. He thought about her often, something he never told anyone. He never told his family what happened with Valencia and they never asked. He could see relief on his father's face when he told them who he was taking to the prom and when they never saw Valencia again, he could sense his father was happy about it. He never admitted how right he obviously was. He still had the letter she'd left for him where she told him she was never in love with him and that she was only with him for her way out of what she knew would be a useless future for her because of where she'd come from. She explained that she'd found a guy who had even more money than his family and she was going to be with him forever. She thanked him for the fun times and apologized for using him. Those were the words of a young eighteen-year-old. He wondered what her was like now.

The moment his father brought up Talia and what a great life they would have together, he couldn't help but think about the many times he and Valencia talked about the life they were going to live and the children they were going to have once he made it big. He remembered the words in her letter, but in the back of his mind, he didn't believe any of them. Valencia never talked down about her life, not even once. She didn't have the happiest upbringing, but never did she tell him that her life seemed bleak because of it. The love they shared was real and he knew it, but if she didn't want him, he didn't want to press the issue. One thing he was not lacking was a bevy of girls to choose from. With a touch of West Indian Heritage in his blood, girls threw themselves at him daily and not just those his age, but women, significantly older as well. Still, he loved Valencia and back then, she was the one and still the one he had been unable to forget. He'd dated and been with lots of women in his college years and hadn't been the most faithful to Talia, who was a few years older than him. She was focused on her career goals while he was focused on the next girl he could get to spend the night in his room. He was sowing his wild oats and doing the same as other guys his age.

Talia was great, but he needed more from their relationship if he was going to make it permanent between them. Now, with the draft over and his career on track, he needed to focus on his transition to the team and handling the endorsement deals he would be signing over the next several days.

Shaking off his trip down memory lane, he stood and refocused on the meaning of the day and knew it was time to rejoin his family and friends. Today was a day for celebration, he thought as he exited the room and walked back to the small gathering. Too bad he didn't feel like celebrating.

Five
Present Day

Valencia walked through the airport with her sleeping two-year-old daughter in her arms. She was thankful that Lina had slept through the entire flight and hadn't ruined the experience for everyone on the plane. It was Lina's second time flying and memories of her first trip didn't go well as she cried for most of the flight. The plane's patrons didn't complain about the noise as one woman in her sixties offered to help. Once she took Lina in her arms and played and talked to her, Valencia was surprised when her baby girl laid her head on the woman's chest and went to sleep. Nothing seemed to calm her until the woman reached out for her.

After talking to her throughout the flight, Valencia learned that the woman was a grandmother to sixteen and she knew how to calm a fussing baby. To say she was thankful would be the ultimate understatement. The grandmother, Ms. Ruby, was a god-send. She explained that she spent a lot of time traveling after her husband had passed away four years ago and her children lived in different parts of the country. She loved visiting them often and it helped with the loneliness and solitude that often surrounded her when she was home alone. Lina understood her loss after suffering the loss of her own husband six months ago.

The one thing Valencia never had was grandparents or even parents who really cared about her. She and her siblings had pretty much raised themselves until one day at the age of eighteen, she'd left home and never looked back, until now.

She and Lina were moving back to Miami, Florida to be closer to her brother and sisters whom she'd recently reconnected with after her husband, Harley, who was in the military, had been killed in a car accident after returning home on leave. He and another friend had died instantly when a pickup truck slammed into them at a light. Now that she was again single with a two-year-old daughter, she needed to be around family and her sister invited her and Lina to move in with them. Her plan was to live with them temporarily since financially, she and Lina were not struggling. Harley had life insurance that allowed her to take some time and not worry about looking for a job, while she finished college. Being a military wife for the past four years, she was able to take college courses on line and was now only a few classes away from her degree in childhood education.

After picking up their luggage and exiting the

airport, the Florida heat hit her as she looked up at the bright sun. It was going to be a hot day. She looked around for her sister who was picking them up. Her car and all of their belongings were being shipped to Florida from California, thanks to the military.

"Val!"

Valencia turned at the sound of her sister's voice and saw her running full speed, as fast as she could in high-heels. When she reached them, they threw their arms around each other and tears flowed.

"Aimee," Valencia cried as she held on tight.

"It's good to finally see you and to have you home. How was the flight?" Aimee asked.

"Not bad. Lina slept the whole time, surprisingly. She's had a fever lately and hasn't been sleeping well since Harley's death and I think she was just exhausted."

Aimee leaned back and looked at her niece.

"She is adorable, even more so in person than in pictures and video. Let me take her from you as we walk to the car. Is that all your luggage?"

Valencia took a moment to check and double check the number of bags. She'd brought with them as much as she could carry.

"Yes, for now. The rest is arriving tomorrow along with everything else we own."

"Okay, I did get the storage unit for your furniture like you asked and remember that spare bedroom is yours for as long as you need it. You can either put Lina in the room with you or she can room with Lucia, my baby girl who would love to have Lina in her room with her to play with. It will keep her from asking Marco and me when is she having a little sister."

Valencia laughed because she knew after having two children already, her sister wasn't thinking of having anymore. She, herself, wanted to have many more, but the car accident put a halt to the plans she'd had of having more children. She missed Harley, but they had to now move on. Harley had been gone for six months now and she was finally getting back to herself.

"Are you sure we're not causing any problems staying with you for a while? I don't want to overcrowd you."

Aimee shook her head.

"Nonsense. Marco said the same thing I'm saying to you and that is, we are family and we're here for you as long as you need. We live in that big house and there's plenty of room. Besides, I want to have you close. We can finally reconnect and not just on the phone."

"Okay, as long as you don't mind. Are Terry and Rosita here?" she asked.

Terry and Rosita were their brother and sister and Valencia hadn't seen them since she'd left home many years ago. She was the oldest and felt bad about leaving them with a mother who spent more time in the streets than at home and with a man who was more of a sperm donor than an actual father. Their father, Julio, was never around unless it meant spending the little bit of money their mother received for them each month for food and clothing. When their money ran out, he'd move on to another one of the women he'd had other children by, so many she can't even remember the last count.

One day, her father had somehow come into some money and when she discovered he paid someone to ruin her relationship with Ethan Bennett, she left home. She didn't know where he got the money from, but all she could think about was how wretched of a person did her father have to be to pimp his own daughter out to someone. He'd told her the guy was from Mexico and they needed some photos to send home to his family so that they would believe he was making a life for himself. She agreed and took a few pictures with him, but then realized the guy was a creep. The day that she packed her bags and left home, it was after Julio told her the truth. He revealed that it was Ethan and his father's plan to get her to stay away from him and he did it because he needed the money. She couldn't believe Ethan would do such a thing when all he had to do was tell her that he didn't want to see her again. She wasn't after anything other than his love, but clearly, he and his father thought otherwise and wanted her out of their lives.

After their deception, she couldn't take it anymore. She packed everything that was hers and stayed with a friend for a few weeks until she finished high school. Having nothing to her name, she moved to Fort Lauderdale, taking a job at a hotel she'd heard was hiring.

Two years after graduation, she met Harley when he

and some friends were in Fort Lauderdale staying at the hotel where she worked. Over time, his love and devotion helped her get over the sad plight that was her life.

Harley was six years older than her and was more stable than most men she knew who'd shown interest in her. They continued their relationship and he flew into Fort Lauderdale as often as he could. After spending another two years in a long-distance relationship and her working one endless job after another trying to make ends meet, he asked her to join him in California. After taking a few weeks too long to respond, she looked up one day and he was standing in the lobby of the hotel where she worked as a manager at the front desk. He only had a few hours in town before he had to return to the air force base in California where he was stationed. He proposed to her on the spot and four weeks later, she was on her first flight ever, to California and she never looked back.

They lived a good life and though Harley was gone a lot, he came home whenever he had leave. Two years later, when she told him she was pregnant with Lina, he was over the moon with happiness. He knew what she'd gone through back in Florida with her father, Ethan and his dad and what they'd done to her. He promised her he would love her forever and she would never have to worry about how deep his love went for her because it was bottomless.

Now, at twenty-seven and returning to her roots, she missed him and the life in California he was able to help her escape to. Every time she looked at Lina, she saw everything about him.

Valencia zoned back into the conversation with her sister just as they reached the car.

"Did you hear me?" Aimee said. "What are you daydreaming about?"

"Oh, I'm sorry. What did you say?"

"I said Terry and Rosita are both coming over today. Terry is driving in from Orlando and Rosita lives a few blocks from me. They're both doing well despite our upbringing."

Valencia looked at the fancy car Aimee was driving.

"I see they aren't the only one's doing well for themselves. I love this car."

"Thank you. It's from Marco's dealership. He's about to open his third Lexus dealership and this was my gift for always having his back."

"I'm glad you're happy and doing good," Valencia said. "I have always wanted that for you," she added.

"So are you. I'm sorry to hear about Harley and I wish I had the chance to meet him before the accident. I was looking forward to the family vacation we were planning before all that happened. How has Lina been? I know she's still very young."

Valencia looked at Lina who was still sound asleep.

"She's doing fine and she misses him. She walks around looking for him all the time. They would play hide and seek and I would catch her looking around to see if he would pop out. That was one reason I needed to get out of that house. I think the change will be good for her and me."

Taking Lina from Aimee's arms, she put her into the car seat in the back and got in the car.

"I'm planning a big welcome home party for you with other family and friends. Everyone is excited to see you."

Valencia was burning to ask about their father and didn't know how to bring the subject up. She knew that he had been in contact with her brother and sisters, but she refused to have any relationship with him. Their mother had died a few years ago of a drug overdose.

"It'll be good to see everyone," she said as they pulled away from the airport.

"He won't be there – at the celebration," Aimee said with caution.

Valencia looked over at her and knew that they had been thinking the same thing. "What?" she said.

"Our father won't be at the party. He knows you're coming to Miami to stay with me and I wanted to warn him that unless you ask, he is to stay away from you."

"I'm sorry if I'm ruining the connection the two of you have. I'm just not ready."

"Val, I understand and trust me, that connection isn't that strong. He's done some terrible things to us all and he's still the slick pimp he always thought he was," she said laughing.

Valencia chuckled and was glad that they could laugh about their past. It wasn't the brightest and despite it, they all survived.

"Where is our mother buried?" she asked. Over the

years she thought about reaching out to her mother, but from what she'd heard, her mother had gotten deeper into drugs and wasn't in her right mind.

"Originally she was buried in an unmarked grave because we couldn't afford anything. Two years ago, Terry and I paid to have her moved to a cemetery not far from where I live. I can take you if you want to see where it is."

"I'd like to do that, so thanks. She wasn't the best mother, but she tried with what she had."

"She did and I don't think she ever got over you leaving. Before she died, I told her that we were in contact again and she was happy to hear it. She never asked for your number, though I know she wanted to. She had many regrets about us and knowing you were happy in California, she gave you your space."

Valencia was no longer upset over thoughts and talks about her past. She was looking forward to moving forward with only glimpses into her past.

"She tried and that's all we could have asked for. I had regrets about leaving you kids with her when I left, but I couldn't look after you when I was only eighteen and barely surviving myself. I'm glad there are no hard feelings about that."

Aimee looked over at her and smiled.

"The money you sent to us through Ms. Baker, the social worker, helped out a lot. I know you don't think it was much, but that money went a long way for me, Terry and Rosita. Now, hush with that feeling sad about leaving. None of us blame you. We love you and you deserved to find a life for yourself. You didn't give birth to us and you weren't responsible for us. Trust me when I tell you, we are all fine today and that's what matters. I'm more concerned about how you are," Aimee said as she whizzed through traffic. "I was relieved when I saw you standing there and I could finally set my eyes on you and get a good sister hug!"

"I'm actually doing really well. I'm just about finished with my classes and all set for graduation right before the school year starts and I'm ready to get into the working world. At twenty-seven, I feel like I should have been hard at work for years. Harley wanted me to focus on my dreams and that was school and taking care of Lina."

"He sounds like he was a good man."

Harley was everything to her and Lina and he was the best man. "He was a good man and he loved us very much. He came into my life at a time when I was still hurting from my childhood crush. He once told me that he fell in love with me because of how passionate I was about being in love."

"Well, I hope you aren't cutting yourself off from finding love again," Aimee said.

"Of course not. Harley wouldn't want that and neither would I. Life is too short to be lived mourning the past and not being able to move into the future. I will always love him and I will make sure Lina always knows how much he loved her. One day, if and when the right man comes along, I'll be open to love again. Until then, I'm going to work at being happy."

"Good for you," Aimee said as they pulled into the driveway at her house.

Valencia looked out the car window at the large, beautiful house. "I'll get Lina and then come back to get the luggage."

"I'll get Lina and you get the luggage," Aimee said, smiling.

"Okay. Your home is lovely."

"Thank you and it's your home now too, for as long as you're here and that is dependent upon you. Can I ask you a personal question and if I'm out of line, just tell me, okay?"

Valencia looked at her questionably as she lifted Lina up without waking her.

"Ask away," she said.

"Do you ever think about Ethan Bennett? I know you were talking about him in the car when you mentioned your childhood crush. I hear he's the number one player in the country right now, playing out of Denver. You can't help, but see his face and name on billboards, magazines, all over the internet and Marco loves those damn hats from *E-Ben*, Ethan's clothing line. I thought about you and him while I waited for you at the airport. I don't want you to think that I was wondering what life would have been like if you had stayed together. I was thinking about how in love I thought the two of you were and how you never told any of us what happened between you. His family still lives here and during the off-season, like now, he spends some of his time here in Miami. You may or may not end up running into him now that you're back."

An image of Ethan flashed across her mind. Valencia would be lying if she said she never thought about him. She thought about him often and the hurt of what ended their relationship died away a long time ago. She was happy to see his career take off and when she watched basketball, which she loved to do, she always cheered for him. She was happy that he was happy and it looked like they had each come into their own.

"I think of him often and like you said, he is all over the place, so you can't help, but see him. I hear he never got married, which is sad because I know how much having his own family meant to him."

"He was dating this lawyer lady named Talia for a few years and I hear they broke up about two years ago and she's already engaged to marry someone else. I guess she was tired of waiting around for him to ask her," Aimee said.

"According to the media, Ethan is not starving when it comes to female attention." Thinking back to their time together and remembering their first time together, she knew that he was loving and passionate and any woman would be lucky to have him.

The first time they'd been intimate, he was loving and concerned about her and not rushing to satisfy himself. It took her a few times to have her first orgasm and he worked hard at making sure she was just as satisfied as he was. She still didn't understand their break-up and why he and his father would pay her father to help end their relationship, but it was now water under the bridge. "I'm glad his career has skyrocketed and I have no hard feelings – I wish him well," she added.

"Well, he's still fine as ever. That brother is a walking male model, oozing sexiness all over the place and leaving a trail of broken hearts wherever he goes."

"Yes, he is. He has always been that. Let's get Lina out of the heat. I thought Cali was hot. Until I stepped out of the airport, I had forgotten how humid Miami can be."

"Let's get some lunch and indulge in more girl-talk before Lina wakes and my house gets busy with Marco and the kids," Aimee said.

Valencia smiled.

She was home again.

Six

"Ethan! You're home!"

Ethan smiled and lifted his mother up off of her feet and into his arms. Nothing beat the excited rush he felt whenever he returned home to Florida. Playing basketball for most of the year, he only got the chance to see her when she came to his games, especially all of his games in Florida. She would be at every game and had no problem proudly wearing his Denver jersey. She loved Florida, but she loved her son more.

"Hey, my favorite lady!" he exclaimed, hugging her and covering her face with kisses.

"I wasn't sure if you were coming here before heading to Baltimore to visit your brother."

Ethan always took time during his off-season to go to as many of Eli's baseball games as he could. "I'm going to Baltimore in about a week for his back to back games. I hope you and Pop don't mind me intruding on your territory for a few weeks since I'll be in and out in search of home-cooked meals. I miss you. The season starts back up in October and I have to report for training in September. I also want to spend a few days in Paris with Esha before the season jumps off."

"Ah, I see you're making your rounds. I also see you've come home alone, or did you? Where's Aubrey?" Moriah said, looking around as if she were expecting Aubrey to suddenly appear.

Ethan should have expected the conversation would turn to the last woman his mother knew him to be involved with. It was hard for him to tell her that none of the women were anything serious, just pretty much bed warmers. That's not a conversation one has with his mother. He did like Aubrey, but they'd started dating in the heat of his season and she had a hard time dealing with him being on the road all the time. Of course, like with most women he dated, jealousy played a hand in the end of their relationship.

"Mom, you know I'm not dating Aubrey exclusively and if I brought her home, that would send the wrong signal. When I bring a woman home, you'll know it's serious. I'm twenty-seven and I still have many years ahead of me to fall in love, get married and surround you with more grandchildren than you'll be able to keep up with," he quipped.

Moriah laughed. "Well, as long as grandchildren are in my future, I won't push. You know that's not me. All I want is for you to be happy and to know that there is more to life than playing basketball and endorsement deals. One day, I'd like to see my son with one woman on his arm and not the hundreds of different ones I see in images all the time."

"Hundreds, mom? Really? Stop reading stories about me in the media. I don't give many interviews and you know that. A lot of that is what they create to sell magazines. If there is anything about me that you want to know, ask me. Unlike them, you have direct access to me at all times. Where's Pop?"

"He's just leaving the office and is on his way here. We were planning on going out on the boat with some friends this evening, but now that you're home, we can do that another day and cancel our plans."

"No, don't do that. Go have fun with your friends. I'm hanging out with a few players tonight anyway. We're going to a baseball game and then out for drinks at a club later."

Ethan laughed when she looked at him suspiciously. "Do I need to ask what kind of club?" Moriah asked.

"I'm not going to a stripper club, mom. Not all guys my age do that, though I have been. You do remember that I am part owner in a nightclub here and that's where I'm heading later. I'm in Miami to chill as much as I can after the winning season. I've been from the final winning game, to the White House, to my home in Denver and now here. I'm looking forward to relaxing and chilling. I am hoping to get a some of Ms. Hattie's cupcakes. Is she here?" he asked.

Ms. Hattie has been their cook since he was a little boy running around in diapers and she made the best cupcakes.

"She is and as soon as she hears you're here, she'll start rummaging through the cabinets to whip up all of your favorite things, including those chocolate cupcakes you love. She's out back resting by the pool. Why don't you go out and say hello while I get a shower and change out of these workout clothes?"

Ethan whistled at his mother as he spun her around.

"Still working out every day?" Ethan asked. His mother loved the gym and maintained great physical shape that even women his age wished they had.

"Of course. I'm still the sexiest woman your father ever met," she laughed.

"T.M.I. mom. That's way too much information for me!" he laughed and went in search of Hattie.

~~

"It's a baseball game, Val. I know you could use the night out and my sister-in-law will gladly look after Lina while she watches Lucia and Teemo. You've been here a week, settled in and now it's time for a little outing."

Valencia looked at Aimee as she tried convincing her that they needed a night out. As soon as she mentioned her three-year-old niece Lucia and her one-year-old nephew Teemo, she lit up. She was already in love with both of them. After being in Florida for a week, Lina was making herself at home and she loved playing with Lucia. She was planning on signing Lina up for the same daycare where Lucia and Teemo went during the week as she finished up school and started her job hunt. She needed to get Lina more interaction with other kids, something she was already used to from their time in California. Though she kept Lina home with her most days, she did allow her to go to the local center two days a week for activities with other children. It helped with teaching her to share.

"I don't know, Aimee, a baseball game? When did you become a baseball lover?" she asked.

"I love going for the comradery and the food. I thought it would be something fun to do and then we could go out to grab dinner, giving us both a break for the evening. My sister-in-law is spending the night anyway and Teemo and Lucia love having her around. What do you say?" Aimee asked, practically begging.

Valencia knew she could use an evening out. "Sure, let's do that. After unpacking all week and getting everything settled at the storage unit, a night out would be good and a baseball game would be fun," she said.

"Great and I've already bought you a jersey and a hat with the number of my favorite player and when you see him, he'll be your favorite player, too. He's sexy!" she shouted.

Valencia put her hand over her mouth to contain the laughter. "Okay, married woman."

Aimee rolled her eyes, winked and smiled.

"Hey, I may be married, but that didn't blind me to a fine man when I see one. Marco loves when I come home at night all hot and bothered after seeing a hot man. He knows he's the only person reaping the benefit of that!" she wisecracked.

"I am really enjoying being back home in Florida around everyone and that party last night was crazy and wild. Having Terry and Rosita here all week has been the best. I'm sorry Terry had to get back to Orlando. Is Rosita going to the game with us?"

"No, she's hanging out with some friends tonight. Her boyfriend got some kind of promotion at work and they're going out to celebrate."

Valencia could barely contain her excitement when she looked around the room at the party Aimee had thrown for her return and she had her brother and sisters in one room again.

"Look at us, me at twenty-seven, you at twenty-five, Rosita at twenty-three and Terry at twenty-two all doing great," Valencia said, happy that they were all connected again.

Valencia watched Lina playing in the baby pool with Lucia and Teemo and she knew coming to Florida was the best choice for them. Except for friends she'd made in California, she didn't have anyone else there and the place started to get lonely. While staying in touch with Ms. Ruby, she was happy when she looked up the day of the funeral and saw her in attendance. She stayed a week to help her with Lina before heading back out to visit one of her children. Now, to see Lina happy and playing, she knew moving was the best move for them. She relaxed when she saw how much fun Lina was having as Aimee's sister-in-law, Vicki looked after the kids in the pool.

"Did you finish going through everything that was

shipped here? I told you I would help," Aimee said.

"I know you offered and I was planning to go through everything once I got here, but Harley's mother and sister came out to California and we went through his things together. I kept the things I wanted most like pictures and other sentimental things and they agreed to take care of his clothes and other items. I didn't do much other than make sure everything arrived. I gave his motorcycle to his brother and he flew out to California to pick it up and drove it back to Vegas where he lives. It was time and that saved me a lot that I didn't have to pack."

"Is his family good to you?" Aimee asked.

"They are the best and Lina loves her grandma. His sister had become like another sister to me and his brother was another protector. I told them anytime they wanted to see Lina, they could come visit and for the Christmas holiday this year, I'm going to let her spend two weeks with his family in Philadelphia. I want to be sure she stays in close contact with Harley's family. I didn't understand how important family was until I met him and he was the reason I reached out to you and reconnected. He told me I was doing myself and you an injustice by staying away with no contact even though I told him I had let you all know that I was alive and doing okay after I left. The day that I got that first phone call from you after writing and putting my phone number in a letter, was a major turning point in my life. Losing Harley, I know how important each day with family is. I also know that living every day to the fullest is important. There were many things he and I wanted to do that we never got the chance to do and from him I learned to go for what I want."

"Well, I never got to meet my brother-in-law in person, but I enjoyed my phone chats with him and he made you happy and that made me love him even more. How is your heart? Is it healing?" Aimee asked.

Valencia didn't know how to answer that. She missed her husband and the love they shared and she knew that she would forever miss him. Knowing Harley the way that she did, she had no doubt that he wouldn't want her to live the rest of her life never experiencing love again because he loved her that much.

"My heart is healing, I miss him all the time and I needed this new start. He was everything to me and that kind of love doesn't come around too often."

"He was your first love, so I know how you feel," Aimee said.

Valencia looked at her and contemplated her next words. She would never overshadow the love she had for Harley, but the truth is, Harley wasn't her first love.

"Harley wasn't my first love, Aimee; Ethan was."

"I know and I'm sorry for saying that. I would never play down your first love. I guess I saw your love as everlasting with Harley, which is more of what I meant. I know that your love, back then for Ethan, was as real as love could get."

"Things didn't work out between us, but Ethan will always be my first love. Do you know that the night I met Ethan, we went out with a bunch of people after a pickup basketball game and had burgers and fries and this jukebox was playing "Endless Love", that song by Diana Ross and Luther Vandross? One day, weeks later, Ethan remembered that, though I didn't and he told me he would never forget the day we met because he fell in love that day and that song playing was his confirmation. I never forgot that," she said. She didn't admit that she never stopped thinking about the love they shared and for years, it bothered her that they never really had closure.

"Are you ever going to tell me what happened? The two of you were inseparable back then," Aimee asked.

No one needed to know, Valencia thought. She didn't have a relationship with their father, but Aimee and her sister Rosita did. She didn't want to ruin that by rehashing a history that could ruin what they had built over the years with him.

"It's so far in my past, I want to leave it there. It happened and both of us moved on and are living happy lives."

She had kept up with Ethan's personal life, even though it pained her at times to see him with one woman after another. He had been her first everything and the love she shared with Harley helped her heal from the loss of her first love.

"Well, as your sister, it is my job to make sure you don't continue to live in the past, but look forward to a great future. The game is at seven and we have great seats, compliments of my husband's partner who couldn't use the tickets due to a last-minute trip. Marco couldn't use the tickets because of work commitments and gave them to me to take you."

"Did I tell you how awesome your husband is? He and Harley would have loved connecting and drinking over sports."

Aimee nodded in agreement. "I agree with you on that."

"I'm going to get Lina out of the pool for an afternoon nap. I want to give her dinner before we leave for the game."

"I'm going to join you with Lucia. Teemo will go ballistic if we take him out of the pool before he's ready to get out. That boy loves the water," Aimee said standing and heading toward the kids.

"I'm looking forward to our night out and if nothing else, somewhere before the end of the night, I'd like to indulge in a Sangria. I never drink when I have Lina and if I'm going to have a night out that's kid-free, I want to make it count!"

"I'm all for making it count and tonight the world is ours!" Aimee jested as they took the kids inside.

Seven

Ethan walked in front of his security into the private team entrance to the baseball stadium with friends of his who were also pro-basketball players. Competition or not, they had a friendship that bound them as brothers for life and when they were together, he wasn't Denver and they're weren't Florida or New York, but brothers who created a friendship out of their love for playing the game. Around them he could be himself without having to always be Ethan Bennett, star basketball player - with them he was Ethan or E-Ben, the same name he used for his clothing line.

"I think Florida is going to take the baseball game tonight, I can feel it in my bones!" Derek boasted about his hometown team. Like Ethan, he was from Florida though they didn't meet until they played professional basketball for different teams. Anytime he got a break and came back to Florida for a visit with his family, most of the time, he and Ethan hung out since he would be in town visiting his.

"The only time I root for Florida is when my brother isn't on the opposing team and since they aren't playing Baltimore tonight, I'm going with Florida to win, too," Ethan said.

"Both of you are foolish because Chicago is in for the win tonight," Liam added, another pro-basketball player who played in Los Angeles, but loved the Florida night life.

"Are you serious?" Derek asked as they walked through the team only area of the stadium. They were looking forward to meeting up with a few of the players before the game started, a perk of also playing in the professional arena.

"As serious as I can be. I understand that Florida sits at the top right now, but Chicago is about to wipe the floor with them."

"Dude, we're on our way to meet the hometown team players. Don't be all up in there spreading that blasphemy and getting us thrown out!" Ethan chided.

"I'll keep my trash talking until after the game when we hit the club. We are still going, right?" Liam asked.

"The question is, are you still going? You're the one with the wife and kid back at the hotel. Is she letting you out to play late this time? You know the last time, we had to drop you off before curfew ended," Derek joked.

They all laughed just as they reached the locker room. They hadn't gotten far when some of the baseball players recognized Ethan and congratulated him on his best season yet. In his ninth year as a professional player, he had endured his best year with many career highs including another win as MVP for the season. He had just signed one of the largest multi-million-dollar contract extensions in the history of the game, locking him in for the next five years with his team in hopes that he could continue the streak of bringing home the big win.

Over the last nine years, his team had won the championship six times. With the recent draft, his team had acquired some powerhouses straight out of college. He was looking forward to getting back with the team in a few months to prepare for the next season. In the meantime, his mind was on getting some much-needed downtime.

"Are you guys in the skybox for the game?" one of the players asked.

"Of course," Derek answered first. "We can't have this guy out with the general public. We would never be able to enjoy the game," he said pointing to Ethan.

Ethan didn't comment because he knew Derek's words rang true. Whenever he was out, a crowd gathered and though he loved his fans, they forgot that he liked his space just like anyone else, especially during off-season.

"Right, I hear he's the country's most eligible bachelor, still causing wet dreams in women's bedrooms everywhere," another player said.

"Women everywhere will be in mourning the

moment he puts a ring on a woman's finger."

Ethan heard ring and perked up. There hasn't been a woman he wanted to put a ring on it for. Not that they weren't worthy, but he wasn't ready. The only woman he ever thought of as a wife was Valencia Ramos and that had been many years ago. He thought about her often and each time he came home to Florida, he wondered if she still lived in the same area and how her life had turned out. Had she gone to college, gotten married or had any children? That was the life they were to have together. He turned his thoughts back to the conversation.

"They'll be waiting to mourn for a long time because that's not happening anytime soon," Ethan said, laughing and walking around and greeting more of the team.

"I hope you are here bringing us some of your luck tonight for our game. We have a few of our best players on the injured list tonight."

"Even with that, Florida is still the best team around, well, except for my brother's team of course," Ethan smirked.

"Of course," Liam added.

"We're going to let you guys finish getting ready for your game. Anyone interested in hanging tonight, we'll be at my club, so come on out and enjoy an evening on me in V.I.P," Ethan said.

He smiled when a round of applause was heard throughout the locker room.

The safest place he knew to hang out, especially

when he was in town, was a nightclub, E-Stablish, that he opened up with a business partner and childhood friend, Reggie. They had played on the same high school basketball team, but instead of going into a career in basketball, Reggie opened up several nightclubs and gyms in the Florida area. E-Stablish was the hottest club in town and whenever he showed up, the line wrapped around the block, something he expected to see later since word had gotten out through the media that he was in town.

"We'll be there," several guys shouted as they left.

Followed by their security, they headed toward the elevator that would take them to the skybox. As they stepped inside the glass enclosed elevator that allowed them to look out over the people coming into the stadium, Ethan had to take a second look when he thought he saw a familiar face – one he hadn't seen in a lot of years. He had just been thinking about her. He held his breath as he tried to get a closer look.

"Ethan? You good? What's going on? You have a weird look on your face," Derek said.

Ethan turned to respond and then turned back to the woman who had captured his gaze. It had to be her, he thought. There was no way he could ever forget her – ever. He was leaning so close to the glass, he could see his breath cascading on it. As the elevator rose and he kept his eyes on her, he had no doubt it was her when she removed the hat from her head and tussled her hair. It was much shorter now than what he remembered and was now brown with streaks of gold running through it, but it was definitely her.

"Ethan?" a member of his security team said, also trying to figure out what was going on with him. This time he held his hand up hoping everybody would give him a minute. He was either having the best mirage of his life or the most beautiful woman he'd ever known was in the stadium, closer to him than she'd been in nine years.

He watched as she turned in the direction of the elevator and though she wasn't looking his way, he saw her dead on, leaving no doubt that she was indeed the woman he thought she was; it was his first love, Valencia Ramos. Without thinking twice, he knew he needed to get out of the elevator, even though it was still climbing higher and higher away from her. There was no time for thinking whether or not approaching her would be a good idea, he was going to do it anyway. He needed to catch up to her in the crowd of people entering the stadium before she disappeared out of sight. He watched her stop at one of the food counters and turned to his security.

"See that woman in the white jeans and bright yellow top?" he said, pointing her out.

"Ah," Derek said. "I should have known it was a woman and from what I see, she is gorgeous. No wonder you're acting all strange."

"No, I know her. That's Valencia Ramos, live and in living color right here in the stadium."

"Valencia Ramos?" one of the guys on the security team asked.

"Really?" Derek said turning to look at her again. "That's the infamous Valencia? The woman who broke the superstar's heart? You guys don't know it, but that is thee woman as far as Ethan is concerned. Are you sure it's her?" he asked.

"I know it is." Ethan turned to Kenneth, the point on his security detail for the night while pushing the button for the next floor hoping he'd pushed it in time for it to stop on the next floor. He needed to get off. "Ken, I need you to find her for me if she walks away. Don't approach her, just find her while I figure out how to connect with her without a stampede ensuing that typically happens when people recognize me. I'm tripling the salary for tonight for all three of you if you keep your eyes on her for me and don't let her escape without me being able to talk to her."

As the elevator jerked to a stop, Kenneth talked into the radio that would connect him with other members of his team that were incognito throughout the stadium. Keeping Ethan safe was his number one priority and anything he was asked to do, he did everything in his power to make it happen.

"All ears on level one, chime in," he said. "I got this covered Ethan. Dwight, stay with Ethan, you two come with me," Kenneth said exiting the elevator the moment the door opened.

Ethan stood, still practically holding his breath waiting to see what Kenneth would do as he watched him head toward the stairs. Not wanting to wait, he followed behind Kenneth, hoping someone in the security detail could get their eyes on Valencia. Luckily, there were four other men who were a part of the security detail for the evening on each floor of the stadium at the elevator that lead to the skybox. Giving her description to the one on the first floor, Kenneth gave instructions to whoever set eyes on her first. Ethan looked out over the crowd again as he again set eyes on Valencia as another guy from the security detail walked near her. He didn't want her to be afraid which is why he didn't want anyone approaching her. His face was always recognizable, but he hoped by pulling his hat further down on his head and donning a pair of sunglasses, he could walk over and talk to her without too much fanfare.

"One of my guys on the expanded detail for the night has her in his sights. She's still at the food stall standing in line," Kenneth said.

"I see her. Is she with anyone?" Ethan asked.

Kenneth checked with his guy. "He says she's talking to the woman that's right behind her, but that's the only person he can see her conversing with at the moment. Do you want him to say anything? Perhaps he can keep her there until you get closer."

"Derek, you guys go ahead up to the skybox. I'm going to go down and try and talk to her."

Without waiting for any kind of a response, Ethan rushed down the remaining stairs as Kenneth kept an eye out for anybody in his path.

Rushing down to level one, Ethan tried to hide from people who were rushing by and the moment he found himself walking up behind her, he was stopped, hesitant about the idea of saying hello. It was an innocent gesture, but the way their relationship ended without a real ending, he wasn't sure he should say anything. Putting his reservations on the side, he went for it.

"Valencia?" he said right behind her.

When she turned around, nothing and no one else existed. She was even more beautiful than he remembered and back then, she was a girl, but now, with the passage of time, she was a drop-dead gorgeous woman. The moment she recognized him, he wasn't sure if she'd be happy to see him or not, but he received his answer the moment she smiled up at him.

"Ethan? Ethan Bennett," she asked.

Eight

Ethan couldn't believe standing before him was Valencia Ramos. He wasn't sure his heart would ever stop racing. He knew it was her the minute he saw her and now here she was, within arms-reach and still as beautiful as ever.

"Wow, how are you? I thought that was you. I saw you just as the elevator began rising," he said.

"You recognized me in the midst of all of these people after all of these years?" she asked.

"I would recognize you anywhere. You were always the most beautiful girl in the world and that sentiment has now extended into womanhood. How have you been?" he asked, looking from her to the person with her who looked familiar.

"I've been great. You may not remember my sister Aimee?" she said pointing.

"I sure do. How are you Aimee?" he asked. "It's been

a long time."

"Yes, it has and I'm better now that we've run into you looking as hot as ever!" she said without batting an eye.

Ethan chuckled out loud. "That's the Aimee I remember. Never one to mince words," he said.

"Haha," Aimee laughed.

Ethan then turned his attention back to Valencia.

"It's been a lot of years and time has been wonderful to you."

"And you, too," she said.

Valencia seemed to glow as he looked at her. She was still much shorter than him at around five-foot-nine, which was her height back when they dated. He couldn't believe his luck that he had been thinking about her and here she was, standing right in front of him.

He was about to say something else as people began to recognize him and his detail had to hold people back as they asked for autographs and pictures with him. Moving further away into a more off the side spot, they conversed more.

"Sorry about that," he said.

"It's okay. You're the number one player in the world and you are noticeable even while trying to hide behind dark glasses and a hat pulled down on your head."

"Yeah, this pretty much happens wherever I go," he said as camera after camera snapped shots of him talking to Valencia and her sister. He moved them out of range of any cameras.

"I was about to join them and ask you for an autograph and a few pictures that I can post on my social media page to brag about knowing you," Aimee joked.

Ethan and Valencia laughed.

"Take all the pictures you like and I don't offer that to everybody. Listen, I have to get to the skybox before we incite a riot," Ethan said as his security edged him to get back to the elevator.

"Ethan?" one of the guys said as a warning.

He heard him, but couldn't let Valencia get away yet.

"I'm not sure where you're sitting, but can I convince the two of you to join me in the skybox to watch the game? I'd love the chance to talk more and catch up. Who would have thought that in this stadium with thousands of people, I would look out and see you?" he said. Right now, he only had eyes for her. He didn't care what happened in the past and could care less what was going to happen in the days to come. He only cared that she was standing in front of him and it was more than coincidence. He wasn't taking a chance that she'd get lost in the crowd and he wouldn't see her again.

Valencia didn't know what to say as Aimee answered for them. "Of course! I hear there is usually a huge, lavish buffet in the skybox," she said.

"There is and if there is something that you want and you don't see it, let me know and I'll have someone run out and get it for you. What do you say? I have to get out of here before my detail drags me off," he pleaded.

Valencia looked from Ethan to Aimee, seeing them both looking at her with pleading eyes and she relented.

"Sure, that would be nice," she said.

"Good. Guys, lead the way," Ethan said and they followed his detail toward the elevator.

No one said another word, except for Aimee who exclaimed how happy she was to be watching the game from the skybox.

"Would they mind if I took pictures in the skybox?" she asked.

"No, but only take pictures that don't have others in them unless you ask. Some guys will be there and the women they are with are not their wives. Be careful with the pictures you take," Ethan warned.

"Do you have a woman we need to know about before we get there? I don't want to have to hurt anyone because my sister will be more beautiful than her!" Aimee asked and then laughed.

Ethan laughed so hard, he had to grab his side.

"Your sister is everything!" he said to Valencia.

"Yeah, she is something. Aimee, if you embarrass me, I will never forgive you," she joked and poked her in the arm.

"Scouts honor," she said. "I promise to be on my best behavior," Aimee said and giggled.

"That doesn't hold any weight since you were never a girl scout," Valencia said.

The moment the elevator stopped, they exited and walked into the skybox.

"Wow! What a view!" Aimee said. "Marco will never believe this. I'm going to take pictures of the field from this location and send them to him. He's going to be jealous!" she hollered.

"Marco?" Ethan asked Valencia as Aimee walked down to the large glass window.

"Marco is her husband. He gave us the tickets for tonight's game. He thought we needed a girl's night out."

"Well, it looks like your sister has no problem making herself at home here. Can I get you a drink?" he asked.

"If they have Sangria, I'd love a glass."

"Sangria it is. If you'd like to have a seat, pick one and I'll join you. Feel free to grab a plate of food."

Valencia smiled as Ethan retreated to the bar and she could finally release the breath she had been holding. Thankful that the air was blowing full-on cool in the room, she didn't have to fan herself, not just because of a heated room, but because she was hot, almost ready to burst into flames. After nine years, she was in Ethan's presence again and there was no tension like she imagined there would be if they ever encountered each other again. Somewhere in the back of her mind, she should have been angry enough about how they ended that the last place she wanted to be was in his presence, but those are the childish thoughts of a young girl, not the mature woman she was now who chose to forgive the actions of a teenage boy. What would be the point of holding a grudge that long? She was happy to see him and it was clear that he was happy to see her. She looked up as Aimee approached, grinning like a kid at Disney World.

"Val, you have to check out the view of the field from here?"

"I will in a bit once the game starts. I'm sure it's amazing. I think we still have about fifteen minutes."

Aimee sat down next to her and leaned over so that no one else could hear them. "So, are you cool with this? I know I answered for both of us, but he looked genuinely excited to see you and he chased you down from an elevator which means he really wanted to talk to you. I didn't think about the awkwardness and I'm sorry."

"Don't you sweat that, I'm cool. I'm not the young teenage girl in love with a boy that I was back then. He may have broken my heart, but it healed and we've both grown up and matured. This box has everything," she said looking around and spotted Ethan walking back in her direction.

"I'm going to get some food. Shall I bring you anything?" Aimee asked.

"I'm good for now. I'll get something once the game starts. Enjoy yourself," she said and turned to Ethan as he sat down beside her. Several of the other guys came over to greet him and he introduced her to the two friends he arrived with.

"It's nice to meet you, Valencia. Liam and I are going

to give the two of you some privacy," Derek said as they walked away. She smiled when she noticed them giving Ethan the thumbs up.

"Your friends didn't have to leave," she said as Ethan handed her the drink.

"Yes, they did or something embarrassing would be said," he quipped and smiled at her.

Before they had a chance to really get into a conversation, they heard the sounds of the national anthem playing and stood. After sitting back down, they focused on the game and chatted about it, staying away from any conversation of a more personal nature since the box filled up with people and Aimee sat with them.

Toward the end, Valencia leaned over to Aimee. "It's getting late and I'd like to leave before the mass exodus once the game is over. Are you ready?" she asked.

"Oh, sure. I'm ready to go. Are you sure you're ready to go? I know you and Ethan have chatted a lot through the game and you seem quite cozy," Aimee whispered.

"We were mostly chatting about the game and some basketball stuff. It's been a fun night, but I don't want to overstay our welcome."

"You're not overstaying your welcome," Ethan leaned over and said.

"Thank you, but we're going to head out. Thanks for inviting us to the skybox. The view of the game from here is great," Valencia said as she stood and pulled Aimee up with her.

"We had a good time and any time you want to

invite us to another skybox, just let me know," she said causing them all to laugh.

"I hope you'll accept an invitation from me again and next time feel free to bring your significant others."

Ethan didn't know how else to get her to tell him if she was involved with someone else or perhaps even married. He saw the wedding band on Aimee's hand, but when he looked at Valencia's, he didn't see one. A lot of women didn't wear them and Valencia could be one of those women. He didn't want her to leave without finding out, but he didn't want to pry.

"My husband would love that and when I tell him about tonight, he is going to be jealous that he didn't get another ticket for him."

"Well, the next time I'm in town and at a game, I hope you both can join me."

When he stood to follow them out, his detail jumped up to follow him.

"Whoa guys. I'm only walking them to the elevator. Go ahead and finish enjoying the game," he said.

Escorting them out of the room and past the security at the door, they walked toward security at the private elevator. He signaled for the guy to open and hold the door for them.

"Thanks again for a great night and it was good seeing you," Valencia said turning to him.

Ethan was glad to hear that because he wanted nothing more than to see her again.

"It was good to see you, too."

"I'll be in the elevator when you're ready," Aimee

said, joining the security guy in the elevator, leaving Ethan and Valencia standing alone.

"Would I be asking too much if I asked you to join me for dinner tomorrow or some other day if tomorrow isn't a good one?" he asked.

Valencia's heart was beating fiercely in her chest. Ethan Bennett was asking her out to dinner. She bit her bottom lip nervously. "Dinner?" she asked.

"Yes, dinner. You know that meal after lunch and the day before breakfast," he said jokingly.

Easing her nervousness, she laughed.

"Well, that is if you don't have a husband or boyfriend at home and if that's the case, I meant no harm," he said, still hopeful that she didn't have either.

"No, I don't have either of those, but I do have a two-year-old daughter at home and I try not to be out too many nights away from her."

"You have a daughter? I bet she's as pretty as her mother."

Valencia smiled. "Thank you. She is the light of my life."

"A daughter, no husband, no boyfriend? Are you sure you can't join me for dinner if I promise not to keep you out late?" he pleaded.

"I'll watch Lina for you and you could use another night out," Aimee said from the elevator.

Valencia turned to Aimee and gave her a scolding look, followed by a genuine smile.

"I love my sister, but there are times when I want to strangle her."

"Listen, I don't want you to do anything you're uncomfortable with. I'd like to give you my number and if you change your mind, give me a call," Ethan said.

This is not hard, Valencia thought to herself. It's just dinner and she would love the chance to see him again.

"Dinner would be great," she said.

Ethan smiled like he'd won the lottery.

"Thank you for saying yes. How about I pick you up around seven? That way I don't keep you out too late away from your daughter."

"Seven is fine."

"Put my number in your phone and when you get a chance, text me the address and I'll see you at seven tomorrow night. I'm looking forward to it," he said.

Valencia added the number he gave her and looked away shyly at his excitement. Inwardly, she was just as excited, but held back. This was Ethan Bennett and he looked at her the same way he had done years ago. Dinner should be interesting, she thought as she turned to walk into the elevator.

Ethan waited until the doors closed before he walked back into the skybox with his thoughts completely on Valencia and how much he was looking forward to seeing her the next night.

"Okay, now that you've climbed back down from cloud nine, do you want to tell me more about that beautiful woman? The look on your face while she was with you spoke volumes. I think you were happier than you were when you won the championship game. Your face said 'winning'! Clearly, she isn't some groupie or passing distraction, but she's more than that," Liam said the minute he entered the room. "Derek mentioned she broke your heart when you were teenagers, but that was all he knew."

Ethan fought with the struggle within knowing the inevitable had happened. The young girl he fell in love with as an eighteen-year-old was now a beautiful twenty-seven-year-old woman and he was still in love. He smiled to himself and looked straight at them.

"That was and still is the love of my life. That, fellas, was the only woman I have ever loved and despite the fact that she broke my heart back in high school, today I realized she still has my heart."

"I haven't heard you say the word love since Talia and even that wasn't a long-lasting love, but looking at the look on your face now, the one we saw when you spotted her and the one we acknowledged throughout the game, you are a goner," Derek said.

Ethan had no problem admitting it to himself and others.

"I think you're right. Let's finish checking out the rest of the game."

Nine

"Ethan!"

Turning Ethan saw Reggie heading his way as he entered the club. After the game, he rode in silence as Derek and Liam chatted about the game. His mind wasn't on the game, but on Valencia instead. To say that he was still in shock would be an underestimate of the fact. As excited as he had been about coming out to the club, all he really wanted to do was see and talk to Valencia. He started to back out of going, but knew he would never hear the end of it from Derek and Liam, so he went along. Now at the club and seeing the large crowd, he was glad he made the decision to show up. He didn't want to miss the chance to catch up with Reggie.

Back in high school, Reggie was his go-to guy on and off the basketball court. They always had each other's backs and they remained the best of friends, though

Ethan's career took him away from Florida for the better part of the year.

After college when Reggie decided to go into club management and the opportunity came where they could partner on several business ventures, he took Reggie up on the offer.

"What's up, bro!" Ethan said as they greeted each other.

"Derek, Liam – good to see you, too. I see you're still hanging out with this fool," Reggie joked.

"Yeah, without us and you, he would be friendless," Derek said. "This place is jumping tonight!"

"I have Ethan's private area all stocked and ready for you. Some of the guys from the baseball team are already here and enjoying the VIP treatment. I have security on the lookout for the others," Reggie said. "Let me steal Ethan for a minute while you guys go do what you usually do. This time, try not to take every woman in the club home," Reggie said, sarcastically.

"I can confirm that I won't, but Derek here probably has a different plan in mind," Liam said. "I don't think the wife would approve of the company," he joked.

"No ball and chain for me, so you know it's on!" Derek declared.

"I'll catch you in a few," Ethan said, following Reggie toward the elevator that would take them up to the office.

"How was the game?" Reggie asked.

"Florida won of course. Great game as always. I would ask how the club was doing, but I can see by the number of people still outside waiting to get in."

"It's been good. I can usually expect a crazy crowd like that when you're in town, but it's been like this for the past few months. I think it's time for a second location."

Ethan had the same idea the minute he pulled up and saw the crowd. There were still a few hundred people outside waiting to get in. "I agree. We can talk through that while I'm in town. Whatever you need from me, let me know," Ethan said.

"That's good to hear. Are you hanging around until the seasons starts back up?"

"Some. I'm going to Baltimore to visit my brother and then a quick trip to Paris to visit with my sister."

"How's the family?" Reggie asked as they entered the office. Ethan took a seat as Reggie went to sit behind his desk.

"The family is good."

"Nobody's married with children yet?"

"No. Esha and Eli are both focused on their careers."

"And you?"

Ethan knew that Reggie knew him better than most people. He knew how much family meant to him and his desire to one day have one of his own.

"Not everybody can be as happily married and in love with their high school sweetheart like you and then to pop out three beautiful children in the past four years. Don't you give Raina time to breathe in between kids?" Ethan joked.

"Whatever she wants, she gets and she loves those

babies almost as much as I do. Lil' Reggie asks about his godfather, Ethan, all the time. He loves watching your games with me."

"You need to actually bring him to one of my games and not just watch it on the tube. You know I would never come to town and not visit them. I'll stop by before heading to Baltimore. We have to get together for a barbecue. I still haven't seen the youngest baby in person yet."

"Well, I'm hoping they won't be too big before you decide to settle down and have a few of your own. We always talked about our kids growing up and becoming best friends like you and I," Reggie said.

Ethan remembered those talks which occurred when they were both dating girls in high school. Back then, he was with Valencia.

"Yeah, well, one day."

"We had a lot of dreams back then and it looks like we both stayed on track."

Ethan couldn't agree more with the only thing that hasn't happened for him was to fall in love and get married. The thought made him think of Valencia.

"Guess who I ran into tonight at the game?" he said with more excitement than he wanted to display.

"Whoever it was must be someone huge because you just perked up like Santa Claus walked in the room or something. Who was it?"

"Valencia Ramos."

Ethan knew he didn't need to say more as he watched the play of emotions that crossed Reggie's face. He was sure Reggie was thinking of the drama that surrounded Valencia back in high school. Reggie was the only person he confided in about the hurt he felt.

"Really? How is she? I've lived here all these years and I've never ran into her."

"I talked to her some during the game and I know that she hasn't lived here since high school. I don't know the whole story, but she's back here with a two-year-old daughter and staying with her sister."

"She has a kid? Wow. How did she look?" Reggie asked.

"As beautiful as ever. I invited her to watch the game with me in the skybox. We didn't talk as much as I would have liked to considering she did come for the game."

"Wow. Valencia Ramos. That's a name I haven't heard you mention in years. You good?"

They looked at each other as the history surrounding Valencia passed between them.

"I'm good. I'm having dinner with her tomorrow night."

Ethan waited for the other shoe to drop once Reggie realized the significance of what he'd just said. "You asked her out?" he finally asked.

"I did and she said yes."

"I know you mentioned a daughter, but is there no husband or boyfriend?"

"She said there wasn't."

"Are you sure you want to do that?"

"Do what? Have dinner with her?" Ethan asked.

"You and I both know how you felt about her and from the look on your face, something tells me those feelings have resurfaced. Is that the path you want to go down after what happened?"

"That was nine years ago and it's just dinner. I want to see what she's been up to all these years. It wasn't just luck that I spotted her in a stadium full of thousands of people. I had been thinking about her moments before that. I look up and there she is."

"It was a chance encounter, Ethan. Are you ready to think of it as more than that?"

Without hesitation, Ethan already knew the answer. "Yes."

"Okay. You know I will always have your back and will always be supportive. Still beautiful, huh?"

"More than she has ever been. She was gorgeous and still has that bright, genuine smile."

"What happened to Aubrey, that sexy little number you were dating?" Reggie asked.

"She couldn't handle my being on the road all the time and brought too much drama."

"So, in other words, she was another woman who wasn't Valencia Ramos. I know you've compared women to her over the years. So far, none has compared, not even Talia who I thought would be the one."

"Do you think dinner is a mistake?" Ethan asked. He had run the idea through his own mind and couldn't come up with a reason to not enjoy a conversation over dinner with her.

"Of course not. Whether it's dinner or more than that, I say go for it. You only live once and life is too short for regrets. Who knows, perhaps there is something in the cards for you and your first love."

"Maybe," Ethan said. He smiled knowing he could always count on Reggie to give it to him like he felt it. His advice and opinion have always been accompanied with honesty. Even at eighteen, Valencia was everything to him and seeing her reminded him that he'd never stopped loving her and if anyone would sympathize with his feelings, it was Reggie.

"My advice is go with your heart. If you have a chance to rekindle something, do it and don't let any past discrepancies keep you from it. She was the woman for you back then. If no one else besides you and I knew that, it didn't matter. She could very well be the woman for you now."

"For now, it's just dinner and two old friends catching up. I can't wait to hear about the past nine years."

Ethan watched as Reggie thought long and hard about his next question. They've always passed things by each other over the years and trusted each other's views.

"What if the incident that broke you up resurfaces? Are you going to finally close that chapter out and address it by getting some answers?"

"I don't know. I don't want it to ruin dinner, but I will say it's something I want to know. You know how much I loved her and it wasn't just teenage or puppy love. She was my first experience with real love."

"I know it was. Maybe you'll get some resolution. If it's going to be more, I'll be the first one happy for you. I'll dance at your wedding!"

Ethan laughed knowing Reggie was trying to keep them from being so serious.

"I know you will. Now, no more talk about Valencia. I want to know about this club expansion. I need to get my mind off of her for a bit and focus on something else before I drive myself crazy."

"Okay, business it is, but you know you're a goner and there is nothing you can do about it."

Ethan gave up. "I think you're right."

Ten

"Mom, are you in here?" Ethan hollered as he walked toward the kitchen.

"Yes, I'm here. I wasn't sure if you were coming back here last night after your night out or if you were going to stay at your house or at your condo."

"I stayed at the condo last night. I wasn't sure if the cleaners would be done getting the house ready for me for the summer. I called ahead to have the condo cleaned, but didn't make the call about the house until last night. It was late when I left the club and I wasn't sure how late you and Pop would be out, so I went home. How was your night out on the boat?" he asked, coming into the kitchen and sitting at the island, looking around.

"I know what you're looking for and Hattie left you a few over on the counter."

Ethan smiled and went in search of the cupcakes

that had his name on them. He watched his mother's look of surprise when he gulped one done in one bite.

"Stop eating like that," she reprimanded.

"These are so good and moist – I couldn't help myself. The boat?" he asked again.

"Oh, yes we had a great time. Your uncle and aunt joined us along with some other friends. We had a nice, relaxing evening. Do you want some milk?" she asked.

"No, I'm good. I'll grab a bottle of water," he said heading for the refrigerator.

"So, how was your night out and what day are you leaving for Baltimore?"

"I'll be here for about a week, but remember I'll be back before visiting Esha in Paris. I think she's in Italy right now."

"Does Eli know you're coming?"

Ethan had to think back to whether he told Eli he was coming or not.

"I think so, but I'll remind him tomorrow."

"How was the game last night?"

"It was good and guess what?" he said excitedly. He was starting to have an issue with how excited he seemed to be when his thoughts turned to Valencia.

She turned in his direction and waited for what was next, but Ethan didn't finish his thought. "Well?"

"Oh, right, you hate guessing games," he jested. "I ran into Valencia Ramos last night at the game."

Moriah turned away quickly to look busy. She didn't want Ethan to see the shocked look on her face, hearing that familiar name from his past.

"Valencia Ramos? Really? How is she doing?" she stammered out. That was a name she wasn't expecting to hear. In all the years since their relationship ended, Ethan had never mentioned her name again. She still awful about how things turned out, now realizing that breakup forever impacted him.

She knew him to be involved with some wonderful women over the years, but none ever made him think of forever. At one time, she thought he and Talia were on the path to marriage, but Ethan never asked her and she finally moved on.

"She's doing good. She recently moved back to this area and has a two-year-old daughter. She is still as beautiful as she was back then, just a lot more mature looking, which is expected after nine years."

"What else did you talk about?" she asked.

She breathed a sigh of relief that they couldn't have talked about what happened years ago because Ethan wasn't fiery mad. He wouldn't be as happy as he was if he knew what happened. It appears it didn't come up.

"Not a whole lot. She is finishing up a degree in childhood education and raising her daughter. We didn't talk about a whole lot of things because we did watch the game."

"You watched the game with her?" Moriah asked.

"Yeah, I invited her and her sister to the skybox to watch with me after I ran into them."

"Well, I'm sure it was good to see her again."

"It was and I'm seeing her again tonight. I asked her out to dinner."

Moriah turned to him and grabbed a cupcake to keep her hands busy to not show her uneasiness. She couldn't shake the past and what her husband had done. There was a possibility that their chickens were returning to hatch and all hell could break loose. It was clear from the exhilaration in Ethan's voice that he still had feelings for her.

"You said she has a daughter. Is there no husband or anything?" She watched as Ethan sat back down and drank an entire bottle of water without stopping in between as she anxiously awaited his response.

"I asked her and she said no. I don't know the situation, but she agreed to have dinner with me. She was gorgeous and though I thought we would be uncomfortable, there was a level of comfort that I think surprised us both."

"So, the past never came up?" Moriah knew that the chance of that happening while having dinner was almost a given.

"No, not once. I don't want to live in the past. It's just a friendly dinner and I see no reason to dredge up the past. It'll be good to see her and again, it's just dinner."

"Are you sure that's it? Just dinner? I hear something else in your voice as you talk about her."

Moriah was concerned. After all of this time, he was about to be one on one with Valencia and she had no doubt the past would come up, even though he said he wanted to leave the past in the past.

"There's always going to be something in my voice

when it comes to Valencia. You remember how I felt about her."

"I do and I know you've also had other relationships including one with Talia whom we all loved and apparently we were the only ones who did. I thought that was leading to something permanent."

Ethan knew his parents wanted to see him marry Talia. She was a great woman and they had fun, but he didn't want marriage when she did and now she was getting that with someone else. It wasn't in the cards for the two of them to be together.

"I know. Everybody thought that, but me. She was and still is an incredible woman who is about to marry the man of her dreams and I'm happy for her. She and I realized the person for her wasn't going to be me and she deserved someone who returned her love."

"Have you been holding a torch for Valencia all of these years?" she asked.

"Until I saw her at the stadium, I never thought so, but yes, I have been holding a torch for her all of these years. I know you and pop and everyone else thought it was teenage love that would go away with time, but it never did, even after our breakup. I couldn't convince any of you back then that my love for her was real. She got me back then like no one else did. Everyone thought she was after something, but I'm telling you she wasn't like that. There was something strange about our breakup that I could never figure out, but that's now history."

"I'm sorry I didn't support the fact that you were in

love with her back then. Like your father, I thought it was simple infatuation and when it didn't last, I assumed that's what it was. What is this now? Are you picking up where you left off? Do you plan on dating her again?" Moriah asked. She tried not to show how uncomfortable she was knowing a secret that he didn't know. She feared what could happen if they got closer and the real truth came out.

Truth was, Ethan didn't know what it was. All he knew was he ran into the only woman he has ever really loved and she agreed to have dinner with him.

"It's just dinner. I'm going to a quick business meeting about the clothing line and I'll call you later."

"I love you, Ethan."

"Love you, too," he said coming around the counter to give her a hug before rushing back out the door. He needed to get out of the house before his mother continued to read more into his reaction while talking about Valencia. It was too soon to tell anyone that seeing her again brought back old feelings and as much as he would like to say he wanted to forget about her and move on, something told him this dinner date was a priority. He would try to avoid the past, but maybe they could finally get real closure. Too much was left unanswered.

~ ~

"How about this?"

Aimee was losing patience with the hundreds of outfits Valencia had tried on for her dinner with Ethan.

"That one looks as nice as the last twenty you tried

on. You said it's just dinner, so why all of this indecisiveness about an outfit? Is there more to you just having dinner with him?" she asked.

"No, it's just dinner."

"Mommy!" Lina screamed from the bed playing in the clothes on the bed.

"Yes, baby?" she answered.

"Mommy looks pretty," Lina said.

"Thank you, baby. Lina is pretty, too."

Lina smiled and played around in the clothes.

"What about how things ended? I assume it wasn't all that bad if you're open to having dinner with him," Aimee said.

"It's been a lot of years and we were kids back then. Sometimes things don't work out. I don't regret anything about my life, including falling in love with Ethan. Those were good and bad times and now we're adults who are having dinner tonight and I need something nice to wear, so help me," she begged.

Aimee looked through the piles of clothes and pulled out a sexy black dress that hugged her curves in all the right places. "A girl can never go wrong with a little black dress and you'll look like a knockout in this one."

"Thanks for watching Lina tonight."

Aimee looked at her with love.

"I will happily watch this little playful munchkin anytime," she said reaching over to pinch Lina's cheek which sent her into a fit of laughter. "I want you to have a nice time tonight, okay? Don't worry about Lina. I'll gather the kids in the family room and we'll watch some movies, probably the one about the stork first. With all the color and excitement in that movie, they'll be mesmerized. We'll have a fun night and Marco is staying in tonight, too. His mouth hung open when I told him who you were having dinner with tonight. I gave him a little history that you dated him back before he was a star and how we ran into him at the game last night and how he asked you out on a date."

Valencia whipped her head around quickly, staring at Aimee.

"Wait, who said anything about a date? We're two old friends having dinner and that's it."

Aimee stood and turned to Lina.

"You want to go with Aunt Mimi? Your mommy is living in a fantasy world if she thinks this is just two old friends having dinner."

Lina jumped in her arms and giggled.

"Don't be snarky because it is dinner and that's it." Valencia wasn't sure who she was trying to convince, herself or her sister.

"I'm going to pick the kids up from my mother-in-law and I'll take Lina with me while you spend the next hour primping for this friendly little dinner. Look at this bed and tell me this is just about two friends having dinner," Aimee said.

Valencia looked at all the clothes from the closet she'd taken out that were piled high on the bed and shook her head at herself. Maybe Aimee was right and this was a date. She sure was acting like she was going out on one. This was Ethan Bennett and they were going to see each other again tonight and for the first time, she had to admit to herself that she was nervous. Were they going to be able to get through a night of talking without bringing up the past and all the hurt? She didn't want to go back in time to when her heart was cut out of her chest, stomped on and burned to pieces.

"It's just dinner, sis," she finally said, convincing them both.

"Keep telling yourself that. I'll put Lina's crib in Lucia's room so you don't wake her when you get in. If you're not coming home tonight, send me a text."

Valencia looked at her stunned.

"Why wouldn't I come home tonight?" she asked.

"Has it been that long? Do I need to give you a lesson that equates to how it's like riding a bike?" Aimee retorted.

"Funny. I don't recommend taking that show on the road." She walked over to Lina. "Give mommy a kiss before you go with Aunt Mimi," she said.

After getting a tight hug around the neck and several kisses, she rushed around to get ready for dinner. Ethan was coming in an hour and she wanted to be ready. They had been texting earlier in the day when she'd sent him her sister's address. He expressed how excited he was about having dinner with her and without any shyness, she told him her excitement matched his. They had exchanged a few other texts and he told her to dress nice because he was taking her someplace really nice. He told her he hoped Italian was still her favorite food and she acknowledged that it was.

"He remembered that," she said out loud to herself since she was alone. Ethan remembered that her favorite food was anything Italian. That made her smile.

Grabbing what she needed, she put her hair under a shower cap and headed for the shower eager about her night.

Eleven

"Ethan pulled up to the address Valencia had given him and was about to get out of the car, when he remembered to grab the bouquet of flowers he'd picked up on his way to her house. Now walking up to the house, he checked out the large eye-appealing and awe-inspiring place with its art deco style. The house had two levels with a two-car garage, a long way from the way they lived as children. He was happy to see that Aimee had done well.

From what he and Valencia had exchanged by way of conversation earlier in the day, she'd told him that Aimee's husband was a partner in several car dealerships and from the looks of the house, he was at the top of his game. She had also mentioned that she and Lina had recently moved to Florida and he assumed it must have been after a breakup with her daughter's father or husband, whichever one she'd had. He wasn't sure, but he wouldn't pry. If she wanted to tell him about her private life, he would listen, but he wouldn't push for information.

Ringing the bell, he waited nervously like a teenager about to pick a girl up for their first date. He surprised himself with the number of times he'd changed his mind about what to wear, finally settling on a black suit with a white shirt opened at the collar. He'd called his barber and had gotten a fresh new cut and shave and even had the detailer come to the house to get his ride fresh and clean for the evening while he was out at a meeting.

Unlike a lot of athletes, he didn't splurge on a fleet of cars when he could only drive one at a time. He loved sports cars and loved the sleek new Mercedes that'd he'd recently acquired and had only driven a few times. Other than his motorcycle and the truck he kept at his condo, those were his main means of transportation when he was in Florida and a lot of times, he used a private car service since he was often accompanied by his security detail. Tonight, he'd given them the evening off and it would be just him and Valencia. It wasn't often that he went any place without them, but tonight, he didn't want a chaperone and no distractions. He'd secured an evening for them where he wouldn't have to worry about anyone disturbing them with requests for pictures and autographs.

He was about to ring the bell again, thinking no one heard it when the door opened and on the other side stood Valencia in the sexiest black dress that appeared to have been made for her curvy body. She still had that hour-glass figure that he loved when they were teenagers though she was more filled out now really showing how sexy she truly was. Her hair, which had been flowing down around her shoulders the night of the game was now pinned up with little tendrils falling around the shape of her face. The green colored shadow above her eyes gave her a dynamite, popping look and mixed with the luminescent coloring on her lips, she looked exquisite. The dazzling silver of her jewelry lit up combined with her black dress.

"You look amazing," he was finally able to get the words out. Looking at her, his tongue felt heavy in his mouth, giving the feeling that he could barely form a few words. Valencia looked up at him, smiled and his heart swelled with desire.

"Thank you. You look nice yourself. Would you like to come in while I grab my purse and phone?" she said moving to the side to let him in.

"Sure. Is your sister and her husband here?" he asked.

"Now, you know if Aimee was here, she would have greeted you at the door before I would have had a chance to. She went to pick up her kids and she took my daughter with her. Marco is probably on his way home from the dealership. They're planning to have a family night in, so they should all be arriving back here soon. Do you want to wait and meet them? I know Marco is going to shoot himself if he misses the chance to meet you in person. He talked about you all morning before he left for work. He couldn't believe we know you."

"I would definitely love to meet him and I hope you extend the invitation to come by again. I think we had better get going, so that I don't keep you out too late. I made a promise last night to get you back here at a decent hour," he said, though he would love to spend the rest of the evening just gazing into her beautiful light brown eyes.

Valencia smiled and was happy that there still wasn't any awkwardness between them. She felt as comfortable around him as she did the night before at the game. They were going to have a nice dinner and that was it. Just two friends catching up on their lives. Why should the night be strange because she was having dinner with the most eligible bachelor in the world whom she happened to know on an intimate level? He was the man that every woman of any age dreamed about sitting across the table from and she was about to casually do so as if it were the most natural thing in the world.

"Well, now that you know where I live, anytime you want to stop by and meet him, just let me know. I have no doubt Marco will make sure he's around. I'm ready," she said.

After activating the alarm system, she locked the door behind them and marveled at the slick black Mercedes that was parked in front of the house. "Nice car. Is that the new one?" she asked. "I lover Mercedes, but I don't recognize the model."

"It was designed just for me and it's a model that's

not out on the streets yet. I've had it about a month and this is only the second time I've driven it. I flew home the day the dealer shipped it to me and I drove it around to get a feel for it. I'm glad you like it. A beautiful car was needed for a beautiful woman tonight. I didn't want you climbing up into my truck, though I could have lifted you into it. I may have to rethink that if I get the pleasure of your company again."

Ethan knew the words sounded more like a man enthralled with a woman and not just two people out to enjoy dinner together, but he didn't care. He wasn't holding any punches about his attraction to her.

"Quite the charmer I see," she said as he helped her get into her side. Once he entered the car and started it up, she put on her seat belt and ran her hand over the dark red leather interior. "So beautiful," she said.

"Yes, you are," Ethan said, looking at her with hunger flowing through every part of his body. "Every man we encounter tonight is going to be jealous of me. You are positively stunning," he said.

"I'm sure wherever we go, women and most men will be checking you out before they check me out," she laughed. "You clean up nice. The Ethan I knew would never be caught dead in a suit. I remember how much you hated that suit jacket your school made you wear."

"I couldn't wait to get out of that jacket every day after school and now, suits have become just as much a part of me as my game," he admitted.

"So, where are we having dinner tonight? I know

you mentioned you remembered I loved Italian."

"I have a special place in mind and don't worry about people interrupting us."

"Does that mean someone won't be coming up to our table and asking for an autograph every time you take a bite? I can't imagine that type of life, always in the media spotlight. I see how people clamor for you at your games and other events. It's a good thing you keep your security around at all times."

"Well, tonight we will have all the privacy we want. I've bought out the second level of the restaurant and it will be you and I. That way, we won't have to worry about interruptions and we can enjoy a meal and catch up. How does that sound?" he asked, starting the car and making a U-turn back out of the court.

"That sounds like a plan."

Ethan stopped at the stop sign and looked over at her.

"Thanks for agreeing to have dinner with me. It's been a long time," he said.

"Yes, it has and thanks for asking."

As they pulled into traffic, Valencia settled back onto the deep red butter leather seats of the car and listened to the sounds of Mary J. Blige as she sang about no more drama. How ironic, she thought.

~~

Moriah walked into Tellis' home office just as he ended a business call. She hadn't had much time to talk to him about Ethan having dinner with Valencia tonight. She mentioned it to him and he brushed it off, but she wanted him to know how much it bothered her.

"Done for the evening?" she asked coming up the front of the redwood and marble topped office desk, trying to make eye contact, but noticed he wasn't trying to do the same thing. She already knew why.

"I am," he answered.

"I thought you were going to be late working at the office tonight. When you left this morning, you said you wouldn't be home until way after dinner and I didn't have Hattie make anything for us. We can go to the country club if you want," she said, buying time with idle chat before bringing up her real reason for coming into his office.

"The country club sounds nice. I'm going to grab a shower and change my clothes," Tellis said while straightening up the loose papers on his desk.

"Can we talk before you do that?"

Tellis finally looked up at her and seeing the serious look on her face, she knew he had an idea of what she wanted to talk about.

"Is this about Ethan and Valencia?" he asked.

"It is. They're having dinner tonight and from the sound of his voice when he stopped by earlier, for him I think it's more than just dinner. When I called you after he left, I told you about my fear of what he could discover tonight. What if they compare notes about what happened and he puts two and two together to find what you did?"

"I have been thinking about that and at this point, there is nothing we can do about it. I suspected over the years that memories of Valencia are why he's never settled down and that's my fault. I knew it then and I know it more now. You were right back then when you said I was responsible for his heart breaking. All I can do is apologize and tell him how sorry I am. I never should have gotten involved in his first love."

Moriah came around to his side of the desk and sat across his lap. She didn't like the downhearted look on his face. They had talked over the years about what happened and when Ethan went on with his life, they decided to leave the past in the past never thinking that the two of them would cross paths like this again.

"Honey, I know you're sorry and I can't say that Ethan will understand, but he's more mature now and after immediate anger, I think it will be okay."

Tellis kissed her sweetly on the lips.

"Thanks for saying that even if it's not true. I'm glad that you halted my attempts to invade in Eli and Esha's personal lives. I don't know what I was thinking back then. Looking back, I see how horrible of a choice I made and to drag Valencia's father into it. I don't know if they ever regained a relationship. I never told you this, but one day her father, Julio, called me on the number I'd given him back then. I wanted to know what happened and it took him weeks to call me back and by then, Ethan had taken someone else to the prom and had never mentioned Valencia to us again."

"What did he finally call and say?"

Tellis felt his heart bleeding for the mayhem he caused.

"He told me that Valencia had found out what really happened. He told her it was Ethan and my scheme and that we paid him money to keep her away from Ethan. She was so hurt that a week later, she packed up and moved out. When he called me later that summer, he hadn't heard from her for months and he blamed me for dragging him into what he called my drama. I don't know what happened after that. I hung up on him and never spoke of it again. He told me I had ruined all their lives and was glad his daughter wasn't connected to us anymore. He told me he would rather be poor and drunk than rich like me and hateful. Those words stuck with me for years," he said and leaned his head down on her shoulder.

Moriah caressed his face and kissed his cheek.

"We will deal with whatever happens after tonight. Together we can handle anything and remember our son loves us. You were wrong for what you did, but it's done and we can't go back. If he plans to begin seeing her again, we will embrace it with open arms. We support our children in every aspect of their lives. This thing with Ethan was a lesson learned and we'll make it through. Let's go have dinner, enjoy our evening and deal with this another time."

"Sounds like a plan. I'll get my shower and I'll be down in a few."

Tellis stood and walked out of his office with his shoulders sagging. He should have known that the wrong he'd done to Ethan would surface one day. His son was never happy in love and he knew it was because he took for granted the love he had for Valencia back then. Why he couldn't see it, he will never know. He'd fallen in love with Moriah around that same age and nothing or no one was going to keep them apart. He would have been devastated if anyone had tried. If Ethan brought anger after finding out, he deserved it. His only hope was that they would be able to move on from it in a positive direction.

Twelve

"While we wait for our meal, tell me what you've been up to all these years?" Ethan said.

After arriving at the restaurant, they were escorted to the second level through a private entrance accessible through the underground parking garage. He didn't mind times when he was photographed going in and out of places and he knew that some celebrities had a love-hate relationship with the media and often screamed at them for taking pictures when they were entering into or leaving out of public places. Being a celebrity of sorts himself, he knew that if they really didn't want to be photographed and encountered time and time again, they wouldn't enter and exit through the front door. Times when he didn't want attention, he paid enough for his privacy that he didn't have to encounter anyone if he didn't want to and the last thing he wanted was for Valencia's life to become front page news because she would be seen with him. He took great care in protecting her privacy from prying eyes tonight.

Once they were settled in and the jazz band he'd personally hired had begun playing, they were seated at the only table in the room, making the scene a very intimate one. The lights in the room were dimmed and there were red roses all around them. His original intent was not to create a romantic setting, but he wanted an intimate setting. From the look of things, he got both and didn't squawk because Valencia smiled radiantly when she saw the setup. When they first entered, he looked for any reaction of a negative nature from her, showing her displeasure for how romantic the atmosphere was and seeing none, he felt like he had acted correctly. He didn't want the evening to be about romance, but about a nice, relaxed time. He loved jazz and remembered that she'd enjoyed it herself. The music was being played softly enough that they were able to enjoy conversing without shouting.

"Well, where do I start?" she pondered out loud.

"Anywhere you want," he said. He would have asked her countless questions, but then he may have asked something that she didn't want to answer and that could put a damper on their dinner. He wanted her to share as much as she wanted to share.

"Okay, well, I told you I have a daughter. Her name is Lina, well her full name is Malina, but I call her Lina and she is the light of my life. I met her father when I was nineteen or twenty. He was in the Air Force and visiting with friends in Fort Lauderdale where I lived."

"You moved to Fort Lauderdale? I didn't know that."

"I moved there that summer after I graduated high school. I needed a change of scenery." Valencia looked across the table at Ethan and wondered if he had already attributed her move to the ending of their relationship. "It was a trying time for me," she said, continuing on. "After a while of dating long distance because he was stationed in California, he asked me to marry him and I moved out there with him."

"You lived in California? Did you love it?" he asked. He liked that she hadn't resolved to living her life solely in the Miami area. Life is meant to be explored beyond the cities where you were born and raised.

"I did. It was lonely at first because he was gone so much, but I made friends quickly and settled in nicely. I had finished high school here in Miami, so when I went to California and wasn't sure what to do with myself in the new surroundings, I decided to take some college classes and started working toward my degree in childhood education until I became pregnant with Lina. Harley, that's Lina's father, was just as excited as I was about having a baby and when she was born, she was our life. About six months ago, while he was home on leave, he was heading home after landing when a truck slammed into the car he was riding in, pushing them into oncoming traffic. Harley and his friend were killed instantly."

Ethan's radar went crazy knowing that she must have been crushed at losing her husband.

"I am so sorry for your loss. When I asked you about

a husband or boyfriend last night, I didn't know," he admitted.

Valencia smiled and touched his hand lightly across the table. There was no way he could have known.

"I hadn't said anything about that last night, so you couldn't have known. It's quite alright. It was a hard, dark time for me, but with the love and support of my sisters and my brother and Harley's family, Lina and I are doing much better and she doesn't ask for him as much as she used to. I made the decision to come back here and be closer to family, not just for me, but for Lina, too. It was the best decision I could have made."

Ethan listened as she told him more about her life including how she reconnected with her family after many years of being away. She then turned the tables on him.

"Now, other than what the world reads about you all over the internet, how have you been? What's been going on in your life? No wife or kids?" she asked. She knew he wasn't married because that would have been plastered all over the news. She also knew that there was a woman in his past name Talia whom people suspected he would one day marry, but to her knowledge, it never happened.

"No wife or kids for me yet, but one day. I love children and I'd love a whole houseful of them. I don't plan to play ball beyond the next five years and I've been building my wealth in preparation for that. Hopefully, my personal life will be just as on track as my professional life by then."

"Right, I've seen your hats on every man and boys head and your other endorsements have made you an incredibly wealthy man."

Ethan smiled knowing that she had been keeping up with his career all these years.

"You've kept up with me, have you?" he asked. "That's nice to know."

Valencia smiled.

"Everyone keeps up with you and that can't be surprising and yes, that does include me. I knew you would make it big and you have."

"You always believed in me, didn't you?" he asked.

Before she had a chance to respond, the first course of their meal arrived in the form of the best smelling Italian wedding soup she'd ever smelled.

"This smells delicious. How did you know about this restaurant?" she asked.

"I know the owner and I've often hosted events here, but I've never rented out just the second floor before. When I called him and asked, he said it was mine and he was comping it to me, something I would never allow. Everyone needs to make a living and not to brag about wealth, but with what I have, I would never want anyone to comp anything for me. I believe that those who have, should and leave comps for those who would love to have, but don't."

"Still the kind-hearted person I remember," she said.

"That's something about me that will never change."

They settled in and after the soup arrived, next came

a house salad with the chef's special recipe dressing followed up by a meal of chicken and shrimp scampi, her favorite Italian dish and this one didn't disappoint either of them.

As they talked and laughed well into the evening, Ethan knew that it was fate that he's spotted her at the stadium. Before the night came to an end, he was hoping he could convince her to go out with him again. He didn't want to just rekindle a long-lost friendship with her; he wanted her. He'd wasted enough time enjoying the wealth and fame that came with being a ballplayer and now he wanted something more in his life and that something more was sitting across the table from him making him laugh with jokes she'd heard at a Kevin Hart show she saw right before coming back to Miami. He missed her laugh, missed her gorgeous face and most of all, he missed how happy she made him feel. He felt a lot like that now. He hoped this was a new beginning for them if they could get beyond their past.

Right before dessert arrived, the band played a tune that was meant to be danced to.

"Would you like to dance?" he asked.

"I'd love to."

Valencia waited as Ethan stood and came around behind her to help her up. After standing, she placed her hand in his as he led her to a spot on the floor. With her hand in his, the moment he pulled her into his arms, her body came alive like never before. Ethan looked good, he smelled good and he was making her feel good. They swayed together to the jazz music and neither said a word. Taking a risk, she knew she shouldn't, but couldn't resist, Valencia leaned back a little and looked up into his handsome face. When he looked down at her with so much passion in his stare and a silent signal letting her know how sexy he found her, she swallowed hard to remove the lump that had formed in her throat. Before she knew what she was doing, she licked her lips from one end to the other and watched Ethan's eyes as they followed her action. Being this close to him was overwhelming and her thoughts turned back to a time when she was first discovering what it meant to be loved and that discovery was made while in his arms. Even with the music playing throughout the room, she thought she'd heard him moan or perhaps, it was her who moaned.

What was going on, she thought. Can it be this easy to fall for someone again after so many years? The moment seemed magical. The mixture of the music, ambiance and the sexiest man she'd ever met in her life in the middle of a scene set for romance and passion wasn't making it easy for her to fight her instant attraction to him. She could blame it on alcohol if she'd had any, but she hadn't. What she was feeling was all her and it was all because of the man who looked at her like he wanted to devour her. Silently, she hoped he would.

Like slow motion, she continued swaying and watched as his face came closer and closer to hers like a scene out of one of those romance novels she loved reading at night after she'd put Lina to bed. Lonely since Harley died, those love stories were a reminder that love still existed and was possible even for her.

Valencia knew what was next and if she didn't want it, now would be the time for her to say. As much as he appeared to desire her from the look on his face, she desired him. She wanted him more than she thought she ever would again. Her eyes darted from his eyes to his lips and then back to his eyes again. Without thinking, she sucked in a breath and licked her lips again trying to moisten them when she felt that all fluid had completely left her body.

"My goodness," Ethan whispered.

"What's wrong?" she asked, still mesmerized by the heat of the moment.

"Nothing's wrong; nothing at all. I'm struggling with my desire to kiss you and I want to beg for your permission, that's how much I want to taste your lips. It's almost like they're calling to me and I'm about to lose all control," he said pulling her as close as he could to his body.

When his heated gaze locked onto hers, she froze in place, not wanting to look away and miss the passion she saw forming. "Would you need my permission if I wanted the kiss as much as you?" she asked. She knew there was no room for bewilderment, only need.

She watched as Ethan's eyes darkened as his intense need for her overwhelmed anything else happening in the room. To her the band disappeared, the tables were gone and all that remained were the two of them in a heated moment that spoke to the strong connection they still had between them.

Ethan's thoughts were transfixed on the sheer magnitude of Valencia's beauty as words came from her mouth that set his entire body on fire. She wanted him to kiss her. He no longer wanted to waver.

Coming the rest of the way, closing the distance between them, his lips touched hers lightly and he was overcome with a dizzy feeling. He touched them with his lips again, holding back from kissing her like a possessed man. He didn't want to go too far and ruin the magical night they'd been having, but he wanted her like he wanted his next breath. It was more than a want – it was more like a necessity. The feeling to deepen the kiss overtook him the moment he felt her soft hand reach up and hold on to his back. The feeling of her wanting to be closer to him encouraged him and he deepened the kiss.

Valencia tasted like everything good in the world. She was sweet and tart at the same time, soft and hard and more desirable than ever and like any other hot-blooded man, he wanted more. As their tongues dueled, he reached up and caressed the back of her neck swirling his tongue in her mouth, mimicking his deepest desire for her and she didn't disappoint. It would be okay with him if they never stopped kissing and kept this up until the end of time. If he never had another achievement in his life, this moment with her just topped the list.

After what seemed an eternity, that still wasn't long

enough, he pulled back when he felt the need to breathe. Seeing her thoroughly kissed lips and the look of need in her eyes, he knew he wanted more, but it was time to pull back. He didn't want her think that their time together having dinner had any other purpose other than spending time catching up.

"Maybe we should finish dessert," Valencia said, not sure what to do next. They were standing in the middle of the floor, neither of them making a move to step away and now that she had been methodically kissed, she wasn't sure what else to do to break the trance they seemed to be caught up in.

"If that kiss was out of line, I'm sorry," Ethan said. He couldn't read her to determine if he had gone too far or not.

"No, it wasn't. I told you I wanted it as much as you did, but I think we both can feel that a kiss wouldn't be enough and level heads need to prevail. Agreed?" she asked and smiled to let him know everything was okay.

"Yes, agreed. Let's dive into this pie because it looked good the moment he placed it on the table."

Just like that the awkwardness that started to creep in after the kiss had disappeared. They were back to enjoying the evening without the kiss hanging over them like the thing that wouldn't leave them so that they could get back to a comfortable place.

"This entire evening has been wonderful and I've enjoyed catching up with you. Thanks for sharing your dessert with me. I didn't want to waste mine. I'll take it home and share it with Lina tomorrow."

"I'm glad you agreed to have dinner with me and as I promised, I'm going to get you back home to your family. Ready to go?" he asked after she said how full she was after eating a few forks full of the delectable delight.

"Yes, I am. I can't believe how much I ate tonight and everything was delicious. I wish I had more room for the rest of this dessert, but I'm stuffed."

After signaling their waiter to box up the leftovers and have them brought down to his car in the garage, Ethan helped Valencia up and they headed out. Tonight, had been one of the best nights of his life and he hoped it wouldn't be the last one they shared.

Thirteen

As they drove through the Miami night traffic listening to the sultry sounds of Ledisi, Ethan was still focused on the kiss they shared and how memories flooded through him of the time years ago when he'd last kissed her. He looked over at Valencia at the very moment that she yawned and he laughed.

"I'm so sorry. I don't know where that came from," she said embarrassed.

"Is that a signal to me that you're already bored being around me?" he asked.

"Not at all. Being with you tonight is far from boring. I had a busy day with Lina and she had a restless night after I got in last night. I put her in bed with me and she tossed most of the night, keeping me up. My yawning has nothing to do with you. You are wonderful company."

"That's good to know and I hope I've earned a badge

for another night out for dinner and perhaps a movie can be added next time?"

"You just may have," Valencia said before leaning back, getting comfortable on the ride home. The music was soothing. Ethan must have sensed she needed a moment to lay back and relax as he turned the music up and they rode in silence.

Soon they were pulling up to the house and their night out was coming to an end.

"Thanks again for a fun evening," he said turning the car off and turning to her. All evening, he fought the need to ask her about their breakup many years ago, but after the passionate kiss they'd shared tonight, it was clear that something was still there between them and if he wanted to be honest about seeing her again, that time long ago still lived in the air around them.

"I had a wonderful time." Valencia saw the serious look on his face and wondered what was now bothering him. She knew that look; she remembered that look. She was afraid to ask, thinking he didn't really have as good a time in her company as he said he had.

"I want to ask you something, but I'm not sure where the question will lead and what I don't want is for it to lead to a bad place."

"What's wrong, Ethan? Talk to me," she said turning to give him her full attention. She wasn't in a hurry to get inside. Whatever he had on his mind was important. The street was quiet as the time reached close to eleven. She glanced at the house which was dark. She had no doubt everyone was asleep. Those three kids could tire out the strongest person, she thought.

"The night you broke up with me – why?" he asked.

Valencia stared at him as if he's spoken in a language that she didn't understand. "Wait, what? I didn't break up with you, you broke up with me."

Ethan looked at her mystified. What was she talking about?

"I never did that Valencia. The letter I received from you was clear that you didn't want to be with me and the pictures I saw of you with some guy was the nail in the coffin of our relationship."

Could it be that he didn't know? Could it be that he didn't have anything to do with what her father told her?

"I didn't write you a letter, Ethan. I didn't break up with you and I wasn't with any guy other than you; not until I met my husband. You were my first, he was my second and there has never been anyone else. What pictures are you talking about?"

"I saw some pictures of you hugged up with some guy and he was kissing you on the cheek. I didn't look at the other ones because I didn't want to see. I was furious. Then there was a typed letter that said you didn't want to be with me anyone and didn't know how to tell me which is why you had someone give me the letter. One of my friends showed me the pictures. Who was the guy?"

Valencia thought back to the guy her father had her take pictures with for his family back in Mexico.

"I did take some pictures back then, but they were to help a friend of my father. He was from Mexico and he wanted his family to think that he was living a good life in Miami and that he'd met a beautiful girl. That was staged for their benefit– it wasn't real. I never, ever would have done something like that to you. I loved you and I wouldn't have hurt you like that. Not once when we were together did I even think about another boy. I was all about you until my dad told me that you and your father gave him money to keep me away from you."

"What!" Ethan screamed, forgetting they were sitting in a car on a quiet street late at night. He looked around and hoped he didn't draw the attention of anyone close by.

Valencia sat straight up when she realized they had two different stories of what happened back then.

"My dad showed me a bag of money and said you and your father wanted me to stay away from you because I wasn't good enough for you and the plans you had for yourself. He said you told him I wasn't the kind of girl your parents wanted for you and that they wanted a better caliber of person for their son who was destined to be a star. I never would have walked away from you."

"What the hell!" he said, now enraged. "I have no idea what you're talking about. I never said that and I was never a part of any money being given to your father. I never would have done anything to push you away and don't you think that we were close enough back then that I would have told you? I have never come off as the kind of person who doesn't speak his mind. Whatever was done, trust me it was all my father. I thought a long time about the fact that when I no longer brought you around or even said your name, he and my mother never asked about you. Eli and Esha asked about you all the time and wanted to know what happened, but not my parents."

"Yeah, your father and mine as well. Back then, my father could have been bought with a whistle and a pack of smokes. It's part of the reason we don't have any kind of a relationship today."

Ethan turned to her, almost ashamed to look in her eyes knowing what his father had done because of a preconceived notion of who he thought she was and would be. He sat in silence as he turned and looked straight out the front glass window. The weight of what happened hit him like a ton of bricks. His father had paid Valencia's father to cook up some scheme to break them up so that, in his opinion, Valencia wouldn't be a distraction to stardom for him. He was afraid to speak because thoughts of his father were not pleasant or respectful.

"Breathe Ethan. You have this vein on the side of your head that looks like it's about to pop. I think we now know that our breakup wasn't something either one of us caused."

Ethan heard her, but all he saw was fire. It took him years to get over the end of their relationship and it was all because of his father, not because she didn't want to be with him. How was he supposed to handle that? He did breathe in and out deeply trying to wrap his head around the years of not knowing the truth as well as years of thinking the worst of her. He lowered his head into his hands as he took it all in.

"He destroyed what we had and after all these years, he has never said a word; not one word. He has known all along and said nothing. Earlier today, I had a strange conversation with my mother. She was elusive and that's not like her. I told her I ran into you at the stadium yesterday and that we were having dinner tonight. She couldn't look at me. I think she was worried that the truth would come out over dinner. She looked worried."

"This is all so crazy!" Valencia said, having a hard time taking it all in herself.

The weight of losing Valencia and knowing that his father had a hand in it was making the space inside the car too small for him to think and breathe.

"I need to get out and stretch my legs," he said after having that bomb dropped in his lap. So many things began to make sense. After six months of his life being all about Valencia when they dated, his parents moved on as if Valencia never even existed, not once asking him about her or inquiring about what happened. His father had ruined his life back then and he didn't care. He let his own son hurt and never said a word.

Pacing a few steps back and forth alongside the car, Ethan looked up when Valencia exited the car and came around to his side.

"We can't go back, Ethan. No matter what happened back then, we can't go back."

He stopped pacing and faced her.

"Do you believe me when I say I had no idea any of that happened? Do you believe that I would never have left you like that for any reason? I loved you and even though I knew we came from different backgrounds, that doesn't make someone turn out to be a person another person couldn't love. The moment I saw you on the other side of that fence watching me play ball, I knew you were for me. There was no way I would willingly walk away from you for any reason, not even for a career in basketball. Nothing and no one meant more to me back then than you."

Valencia took him by the hands and held on to them.

"The minute you told me you didn't know, I knew you were telling the truth. I may not like what it looks like your father did, but I understand."

"I'm glad one of us does because I don't and I plan to let him know that first thing in the morning."

"Don't Ethan; don't stir up trouble over something from years ago that we can't go back and have a do-over for. That's over and done with."

Ethan reached out and pulled her closer to him until her head rested on his chest. The minute her arms went around him, he knew that she was right and he didn't need to stir up drama over something from so many years ago.

"I promise, I won't turn it into a drama-filled discussion, but I want him to know that I know what he did and it was wrong. I can't believe he watched me hurt back then and walked around like it was nothing because he had his own dreams for me. I was and still am more than dreams of stardom. I'm more than the athlete I've come to be, even if he was instrumental in making it happen. I'm his son and I should have been more than that to him."

Valencia held him tighter.

"He was afraid that being in love with me, you would make choices based on that love and not on your dreams for yourself."

"I could have had my dreams and you. I didn't have to choose and I don't appreciate that he chose for me."

Valencia leaned back and looked at him.

"Just remember that was nine years ago and right now, we're standing here holding onto each other. You said it was fate that helped you spot me at that stadium full of thousands of people. If you believe that, then you know that there is something more at play here than your father and anything he did years ago that hurt us both. Don't let this draw a wedge in your family because it's not worth it."

Ethan smiled down at her.

"Even now, you are that shoulder for me to lean on like you were back then. You were always the voice of reason when I wanted to go all half-cocked with one idea or another. I loved you so much and then it was over," he said.

"I loved you, too and now that I know that you did and that you had nothing to do with that mess, I'm letting that go and I want you to do the same thing. I know you won't be able to avoid a conversation with your father about all of this, but have it and then let it go. Don't hold on to that anger."

Ethan smiled through the pain of knowing that their lives could have been different, but she was right – they can't go back and change the past, but they could look toward a future if she was open to it.

"Am I crossing a line if I said I'd like to see you again and not just as a casual friend for dinner or a movie? Seeing you again reminded me how much I loved you then and the moment I saw you at the stadium, it was like instantaneous love all over again. I want the chance to see if we could be something and I don't care what anyone else thinks about it other than you, me and Lina," he laughed. When Valencia laughed, the moment was lightened.

"Lina?" she asked.

"Yeah, it's very important that she likes me and if she doesn't, she'll be the only female on this planet that doesn't. I don't want any more time to pass by without seeing what we could be. We let go once and I don't want to do that again now that I have you like this, here in my arms."

Even though it was night, to Valencia the clouds in the sky parted and bright sunshine was shining down on the two of them.

"I'd like that very much and I have no doubt, Lina will love you. You exude a charm that makes you damn near irresistible."

"Well, I look forward to meeting her and laying all of my charm on her from the start. Right now, it's getting pretty late and you need to get inside."

Before they broke apart, Ethan sealed the decision they made to spend more time together and not letting anything or anyone get in the way. He reached down and lifted her chin to bring her lips closer to his and kissed first her top lip, then her lower before kissing along the seam of her lips, eliciting a delightful sound from her lips. The moment she opened them and a sigh escaped, he slipped into her mouth and poured every ounce of passion he could muster up into the kiss, making sure there was no doubt about his intentions. He delighted in the feel of how their mouths mated as the depth of his longing for her deepened. He wanted her to be his and he would give anything in the world to make it happen. Long before he wanted, the kiss ended.

Valencia reached up and traced her lips with her fingers, going across them where his lips had just been. "I see we can't stop kissing each other," she said, eagerly.

"Sweetheart, I know I have no right to think this way after all this time, but if it were up to me, I would love to take this kissing back to my place and spend the rest of the night kissing every single part of your incredible body. That's not the hormones of an eighteen-year-old boy talking. This is from a man who still thinks you are the most beautiful and desirable woman he has ever met. It seems when I'm around you, I can't help that I still feel a closeness to you that I've never had with any other woman, ever."

When she didn't speak, but looked away from him, he figured he had crossed a line and was ready to apologize when she finally turned his way and smiled up at him.

"It's not just me, is it? It's still there. I know what you're feeling because I've been feeling it all night. It's been really hard denying and fighting it and besides, the kissing is amazing," she admitted.

"Yes, it is. I would say it's pretty damn near perfect. You do realize we are standing in the street pretty much devouring each other."

Valencia looked at the house, down at her hands and then back up at him. Her hands were twitching nervously as she struggled between what she really wanted to do as opposed to going inside the house. How could she still feel this way for him after all this time, she thought?

"For a minute, I forgot because all I could do was feel and not think," she admitted.

"Am I wrong for wanting you?" he asked.

Valencia looked him in the eyes. She wasn't ready to fight what she was feeling no more than he was.

"Am I wrong for wanting you, too?" she asked.

Before he could respond, she leaned up as far as her short legs would take her compared to his height and using the aid of her hand, she pulled his head down to her, this time initiating the ardent kiss between them. She went after his lips with raw hunger and the explosive sensation traveled between them, leaving no doubt of what they both wanted and needed. Pulling back and before her level head took control of her strong need to be with him, she went around to the other side of the car, took out her cell phone and dialed Aimee. As she spoke, she never took her eyes off of his as he watched her like a hawk keeping eye over his prey. He wanted her and the feeling was mutual.

"Hey, sis. I know it's late."

"Is everything okay?" Aimee asked.

"Yes, it is. Are you good keeping an eye on Lina for the rest of the night? If not, it's fine and I'll come home."

"I'll do anything as long as you and Ethan don't strip down right in front of my house. I thought I was on the verge of watching a dirty movie," Aimee said and laughed. Valencia turned toward the house and looked up at the master bedroom window.

"You can see me?" she asked.

"Girl, the whole neighborhood can see you and that sexy giant."

Valencia laughed and turned to Ethan who laughed along with her.

"Yeah, I'm a pretty lucky girl to be in the arms of Ethan Bennett," she said.

"He's the lucky one. Go do you. Lina will be fine. She's in the room with Lucia and I'm sure she'll be down for the rest of the night. I kept them up a little past bedtime. If you're having a good time and I hope you are, go have more fun."

"I'll be home early in the morning."

"You will not if that's not what you want to do. Tomorrow is Saturday and I'm thinking of taking the kids out for breakfast and to the park. I'm glad you're having a good time."

"I am."

"See you tomorrow then and tell Ethan I said don't make me hurt him if he screws anything up this time. I expect him to finally get it right."

Valencia laughed and looked over at him again. "I'll tell him, but I have a feeling he already knows and so do I."

She hung up and turned to him.

"So, your sister is spying on us?" he asked.

"Anything is possible with her. Is your place far? I'd like to see it."

Ethan waited a beat before responding.

"Are you sure?" he asked. The last thing he wanted was for them to make a step that she may regret later.

"Are you sure?" she countered.

"I've never been surer of anything in my life."

He didn't question her further as they got back into the car. If she was feeling half of what he was feeling, there was no way they could let the night go by without acting on the feelings they had been fighting all night.

Putting the car in drive, he headed toward his condo in downtown Miami.

Fourteen

Valencia stepped inside of the condo and took a quick glance around. "So, this is where you live? I love it and it's definitely a reflection of your laid-back personality like I remember."

"That part of me has never changed."

After a short ride, Ethan parked in his spot in the underground parking garage and entered the building elevator through his private entrance, only accessible with his key. Once they reached the top floor where his condo was located, the door opened and they walked a few steps to his front door. He had never been more excited to be home before.

"That's good to know. It was one of the reasons I fell in love with you back then. You liked to enjoy life without a lot of fanfare and flashiness, though you could have. I remember your favorite place was the ice cream parlor, nothing big or fancy, just plain vanilla ice cream on a sugar cone," she laughed.

"Guess what? That is still my favorite dessert."

Locking the door behind them, Ethan walked further into the room and turned around. "Would you like a tour?"

Valencia smiled. "I would love a tour. Is this the only place you have in town?" she asked.

"No, I have a house almost an hour away. That's where I go when I really don't want to be bothered by anyone."

"I'm sure it's nice, too."

Ethan grabbed her by the hand and walked toward his favorite room.

"Let's start with my entertainment room and before you ask, yes I'm still a big video gamer. It relaxes my mind especially after a game loss."

Valencia clicked her teeth at him. She had been watching his career closely and knew that he didn't have many losses.

"You haven't had many game losses lately, definitely not in the last couple of seasons," she said.

"You watched me play?"

"You are the number one player in the world right now and I would be lying if I said I didn't marvel like others every time you hit the court. I love watching you play."

"Maybe you'll come to one of my games and cheer me on."

"Maybe I will," she replied quickly.

"Well, as you can see, I still enjoy movies and all other things electronic. I spend most of my time here in front of the television."

"Which one?" Valencia looked around and counted six different sets on the wall.

"All of them. I have to watch every game that's on and they are often played at the same time."

"Right because you hate to miss anything and hate seeing it second hand on the news. That I do remember. Your father had a room at your house back when we dated and it was covered in televisions. We were able to sneak into your house because he would be engrossed in what was on all of those sets at the same time. You are your father's son."

"Not in everything," Ethan said, instantly sending his mind back to their earlier conversation. That quick, his rage returned and as much as he'd like to hide the fact that he was angry at his father from her, he knew that she saw the look of angst on his face.

"Don't, Ethan. There is nothing we can do about it now. I don't want to dwell on it. Both of our lives have come a long way and being angry now won't help a thing. Show me the rest of your place."

Valencia tried to change the mood and hoped Ethan would follow her lead. When he smiled at her and took her hand, she saw a sign of hope.

"The condo has three and a half bathrooms, three bedrooms, the entertainment room, a family room and a kitchen any chef would love to live in," he explained as they moved from one room to the other. "Would you like something to drink? Wine? Water?"

"No, I'm not thirsty. You?" she asked.

The signs were all there that neither wanted to waste time talking or drinking.

Perhaps without knowing it, Ethan saw that Valencia was having a hard time controlling her breathing. All the signs were there that she was as excited as he was and like him, she was trying to contain it.

Ethan's eyes did a perusal of her body and his body heated each time he passed over one luscious curve after another. "I want you," he said without hesitation as he moved in close to her.

"I want you, too. I'm so nervous, I feel like that eighteen-year-old girl again, about to make love with you for the first time."

Ethan let his hands roam over her body, first up and down her arms then around to her back where he traced the curve of her slim waist and over the luscious curve of her hips. Without making her too uncomfortable, he couldn't resist letting his hands travel back to caress the globes of her behind, a backside that would make every Kardashian jealous of its roundness.

He leaned in close to her ear, "in my arms, you don't feel like that shy eighteen-year-old. You feel like a woman who still has all of the curves in all of the right places. You feel like the woman I knew you would feel like if I ever got you in my arms again."

Valencia leaned back and looked up at him.

"You've thought about us like this over the years?" she asked, not surprised because she'd often thought about them this way and wondered how different life and love would be if their path had been different.

"Yes, I've thought about it a lot. There were times when I was focused on the game or other things in my life, but thoughts of you and what your life was like over the years was never far from my mind. I'm still having a hard time believing you're standing here right now in my arms," he said smiling down at her, happier than he's been in a long time.

"I've thought about you, too. I would be lying if I said otherwise."

"I hope you don't think those feelings were wrong. We had something special and I believe it bound us together even though we temporarily took different paths in life."

Taking from his lead, she allowed her hands to reach up and caress his chest through the thin material of his shirt, following the trail of her hands with her eyes. When she encountered strong, powerful muscles, she could only imagine what it would feel like to lay under and over top of him, feeling the steely hardness of his Herculean physique. She let her arms slip on the inside of his and wrapped them around his waist loving how taut, yet strong and virile he felt in her arms.

"I hope the real me is as good as the thoughts of the real me," he said.

Valencia let her eyes drift up to his and her heart began to beat wildly in her chest when his head began to lower down to hers. She wanted and needed the kiss and knew he wouldn't disappoint in its intoxicating impact on her senses.

The moment their lips touched, Valencia felt like she was floating on air with only his strong arms embracing her to keep her from falling back to earth.

His lips were soft, yet rough and the mixture had her yearning for more. When she opened her mouth and he sought out her tongue, their mouths danced with an unhurried lust.

Valencia pulled back first, breathing like she'd seen him do many times when he'd run up and down the basketball court. This kiss was about giving and taking everything and she hoped there was more to come. She looked forward to throwing caution to the wind and going with the flow of their evening together.

"Damn, you taste amazing," Ethan said. "I still feel like I should offer you some wine or bottled water or something and not stand here mauling you in my living room. I know my intention was to most definitely make love to you, but it's not all I've been able to think about when it comes to you. I have no problem admitting how much I've missed you all these years and my love for you never, ever died away. It's always been right here," he said taking her hand and placing it over his heart to show her how deep his love for her still went.

"Maybe I should expect an offer of a bottle of water or a glass of wine, but I don't want either of those right now. All evening, throughout dinner, I've felt the pull to you, the connection I remember we always had for each other and I never wanted to fight it for one second. I'm sure the water and wine will be here later. Right now, all I want is you. You are what I want and I don't think any pretense is necessary."

To prove her point, Valencia stood on the tip of her four-inch heels to show him that the desire was not a one-way street. This time, she took his lips in a breath-taking, power-stealing kiss, filled with everything she was feeling at the moment; a moment she didn't want to let go of. She felt even more the moment he drew her closer against the hard ridge of his readiness and knew that if they didn't soon find a bed, she was going to go stir-crazy.

"A bed," Ethan said breathlessly the moment she released his lips.

"Yes, a bed," she replied and rubbed her fingers lightly across her now plump, deeply kissed lips.

Valencia went willingly into Ethan's arms as he picked her up and braced his strong hips with her thighs. As she crossed her ankles tightly behind his back, not once did they take their eyes off of each other as Ethan walked them into the closest bedroom. Once there, he slid her body down his slowly, making sure she felt how much he wanted her. The moment she encountered his hardness rising thick and long against her womanhood, she knew this would be a night to remember; a night that has been a long time coming.

"There's a bed ahead. Are you sure you're okay with this?" Ethan asked. He had no problem pulling back his desire to make love and spend the evening holding her in his arms.

"I'm here because I want to be and I'm not having

any second thoughts, no doubts and no reservations. I want you," she said, remembering how caring he has always been and that he was thinking about her first, over his desire for her.

She smiled when he pulled her close again for another kiss and walked them back toward the bed until she felt the edge of the mattress against the back of her legs.

"Don't move," he said and gave her another quick kiss on the lips before moving to the wall to turn on a dim light that cast shadows throughout the room.

"I love your room and what size is this bed. I have never seen a bed this big before and it's much larger than a king size."

Valencia took in more of the room and its gray, white and black color scheme. In front of the bed on the wall was a huge television. There wasn't a lot of furniture in the room, most likely, only what he needed and it was all man. The art was masculine in nature and she couldn't wait to take her shoes off to feel the plush gray carpet under her feet.

"It is bigger than a king. With my height, a king wasn't long enough. This was custom made for me. I'm not here often, so it contains the essentials for when I'm here. I'll have to take you out to my house one day. When I'm home for more than a week, that's typically where I am and I would have been headed there this week if I hadn't run into you."

"Well, I'm glad you ran into me."

"So am I," he said coming back over to her after

reaching for a remote that sat on the nightstand. With one push of a button, the room was flooded with music as he searched for a station that played soft, slow R&B music. The moment the sultry sounds of Barry White came across the speakers, the mood was exactly where it needed to be. He pushed another button and panels on both sides of the bed opened and two fire places illuminated the room.

"You still love old R&B, huh?" she asked. Even when they were younger and all of the kids were into rap music, he loved R&B music from the sixties, seventies, eighties and nineties.

"Yes, it's still my favorite and it's what I need to hear right now in between the sounds of making love to you. Are you ready for me?" he asked, moving and swaying to the music.

"I'm just as ready for you as you feel like you are for me," she said, referencing his long hardness, evident in the front of his pants.

Valencia shivered the moment Ethan reached for the thin straps of her dress sliding them down her arms as he kissed a path from her neck down her arms until the dress dropped to the floor at her feet. When his gaze traveled the length of her body, she had never felt sexier as the look of pleasure glowed crossed his face.

"Goodness you are beautiful," he said in a rough, rugged voice.

"I'm glad you like," she said kicking the dress aside and standing before him in a strapless black laced bra and a thin, silk and lace thong. The only other article of clothing were the heels on her feet.

Barely able to breath at the sight of her standing before him looking like a goddess out of a dream, Ethan lifted her up and placed her up on the bed as close to the center as he could get. Once there, he traced the firmness of her thighs, down her legs until he reached the shoes on her feet. Undoing the snaps that held them in place, he slid first one and then the other off of her feet and onto the floor, providing company for her dress that lay in a heap where it fell.

Valencia tried not to show her nervousness and anxiousness to see him naked and it appeared she didn't have to wait too long.

Keeping their eyes locked, she enjoyed the slow striptease he was doing for her, removing his shirt over his head to reveal what her hands had traced earlier, a body that couldn't be sculpted better than his. She could see the ridges of his hard chest and toned abs. She already knew his manhood was long and hard, but her eyes widened when she saw the bulge in his boxers after he slid his pants down his legs.

"Oh my," she uttered, not able to take her eyes off of that part of him as she leaned up on her elbows.

Ethan grinned. "What?" he asked.

"I see something else is no longer that of an eighteen-year-old boy."

Not making her wait any longer to see him in the flesh, Ethan slid his boxers down his legs and removed them along with his pants and shoes. When he stood to his full height, his manhood vibrated when he looked over at Valencia and watched as she stared at his hardness and licked her lips at the same time.

"You're killing me," he muttered in a guttural sound that had the undertones of an animal growling.

"I'm thinking the same thing and hoping I'll be able to walk again," she snickered.

Ethan joined her on the bed and pulled her close to him as he turned them to lay on their sides facing each other.

"I promise not to hurt you and we'll go as slow as you need to go."

"It's been quite a while for me," she admitted.

"I'll be gentle until you don't want me to be. How about that?" he asked, lightening the mood.

Valencia laughed and went into his arms. "I've missed everything about you; your laugh, your smile and most of all being in your arms like this. I'm not sure I appreciated them enough back then, but I do right now," she said.

"Right now, is all that matters. We can't go back, but I'm hoping we can go forward into something special and I'm open to whatever you're ready for. We don't have to talk about it now because I'm laying here naked and you're about to be, but I want you to know that I don't want to lose you in my life again if I don't have to. Don't respond now just in case you're not thinking the same way. I want us to enjoy where we are right now. Is that fair?" he asked.

"Yes, that's fair."

"Great, now to get you to the same state of undress

as me is my goal," he said, moving as close to her as he could get.

Valencia knew the kiss was coming and she was ready for it. She could now feel his skin, hot, hard and moist against hers and her womanhood ached for him.

"Yes, because I'm aching for you, right here," she said, taking his hand and placing it between her legs as the kiss turned even hotter. She moaned the moment his fingers began moving against her through the thin material of her panties.

She closed her eyes as his kiss traveled down her body from her lips to her neck to the tops of her breasts, peaking out at him. She felt the minute he unsnapped it from the back and pulled the cups away allowing her breasts to be free for his pleasure. The feeling of floating on air invaded her body once again, the moment she felt him suckle first one nipple and then the other. He then cupped and kissed around the full globes as his hand left the area between her legs and caressed her hip before he reached for the thin strap, pulling the thong down her legs, tossing it and the bra to the floor.

The moment they were both naked, they rolled from one position to another as they kissed passionately - first on their sides to her being on top and then to him rolling her under him.

"You are so damn beautiful, baby. I've never forgotten how incredibly sexy you have always been. You feel so good laying here under me," Ethan sighed.

Ethan's words aroused her in a way that had her

body grinding in a plea for him to douse the fire that was burning throughout her body. They didn't need the fireplace on because she was generating enough heat to warm up the entire condo.

"I need you, Ethan," she whispered and tossed under him.

"I know. I can feel how hot you are and I need you, too."

Before she could respond, Ethan slid down her body and opened her legs wide until his face was level with her sweet spot. The minute his tongue touched her sensitive nub, Valencia's body instinctively rose from the bed to meet him as she exhaled loudly. She ground her hips feverishly as a rush of moisture flooded from her body while flashes of heat and stars pierced her mind. She was on fire for him.

"Yes!" she screamed and as his tongue worked its magic on her, she flew over the edge into a state of blissful ecstasy while her heart raced and her mouth screamed his name.

Ethan delighted in the feeling of her coming apart in his arms the way he had dreamt about many times since they'd been apart. If he has a say, they won't be apart ever again.

Kissing her inner thigh and moving so that he was positioned at the apex of her thighs, Ethan reached into his nightstand and pulled out a small box of condoms, retrieved the one he needed at the moment and quickly donned it, not sure he'd be able to stand not connecting with her intimately for another second.

Looking down at Valencia whose breath was coming out erratically, he smiled knowing he was able to put that look on her face. With her eyes closed, he knew she was trying to gather herself for what was next.

"You look heavenly with the look of satisfaction on your face. I need to see that look all night," he said, leaning back over her. He positioned himself for entry into her body. "Look at me, Valencia. I never want to forget looking into your eyes at the exact moment that we are intimately connected the way we always should have been.

Valencia slowly opened her eyes, still in a haze of carnality like nothing she'd ever experienced. She'd had so many first with Ethan and the act he'd just performed was something they'd never done back when they dated as teenagers. She was over the moon with wonder at how good he was at it and how quickly he was able to send her over the edge of delight.

With protection in place, Ethan slid slowly into her body while keeping his eyes locked on hers. He held his mouth closed tight when his teeth wanted to clatter. He was trying with all of his might to prolong the encounter. Her tightness was a blessing and a curse. He loved it because he could feel her gripping him as he worked to enter her body, knowing that her tightness made it uncomfortable for her because of his size.

"You're so big," Valencia whispered.

"I'm I hurting you?" he asked and stopped moving.

Valencia's eyes opened wider when he suddenly halted. "Did you stop moving? No, don't stop. It feels good. You're really big and you feel so wonderful. Please don't stop." To prove her point of what she needed and wanted, Valencia pushed up with her hips and then down and then up again, aiding in his entry.

Ethan leaned down and kissed her sweetly over and over.

"Are you sure?" he asked.

"Yes. Love me, Ethan, please," she said.

That was all he needed to hear. Ethan slid further before pulling out and giving her a little more of him each time until finally he entered her all the way and the feeling took his breath away.

"My, my," he said as he began to make love to her slowly, adding a slow, penetrating grind to his hips. When her body was more apt to receiving him, he increased the pace as his erection, thick and long helped him reacquaint himself with her body. Her body felt wonderful as a dizzying feeling heightened his need for her as she writhed around under him, calling his name and letting him know how good he was making her feel.

Their bodies swayed together to the even pace of their love making, causing a rhythmic sound only heard between the two of them, two lovers whose hearts were beating to a pattern that only two lovers who have always had the kind of connection that they had could experience.

"Ethan," she moaned his name.

"Here I am, baby. I'm right here with you," he said as he stroked her body and set aflame the embers that were about to send them into ecstasy together.

With her eyes brimming with tears, her heart racing with excitement and her body humming with pleasure, Valencia let go and gave into an orgasm so strong, she thrashed about wildly under Ethan, screaming his name over and over as she flew apart in a million pieces.

Ethan fought the urge to drill into her relentlessly as his body gave into the pleasure. His own climax slammed into him and hurled him around as if he were in the midst of a tidal wave. His body shuddered one time, a second time and then continued with no end in sight. His legs grew weak as they shook from the magnitude of the explosion flowing through him. When Valencia's body began to calm, his climax began to subside and he only had enough strength to move to the side of her to not put his full weight on her as he waited for his heart rate to return to normal.

He continued to ply soft kisses on her now moist skins, slick with perspiration from their amorous movements while at the same time, his mind was flooded with words and thoughts of thankfulness that he was back where he belonged - in the arms of the only woman he ever really loved; his first love.

Fifteen

"Text me when you get back home. I want to know you got in okay because you have to be exhausted being up all night and then driving me back here," Valencia said as they walked to the trunk to get the dessert that she was glad they remembered to take out the night before and place in his fridge.

She yawned after getting no sleep. She and Ethan were like two sex-crazed lovers who couldn't keep their hands off of each other. When she thought sleep was about to overtake her, she would feel Ethan's soft caress on some part of her body and she was again aroused to the point where she needed to feel him again as much as he needed to feel her. It was a night filled with him reaching out for her or her reaching out for him and they gave in to the crave for each other every single time.

Now in the early hours of the morning, before the sun was even up, she wanted to get back to the house before Lina woke up and began looking for her.

"I will and thanks for an incredible evening. I know we didn't set out to end up in bed, but I will never have regrets about it as I hope you won't. We still need to talk because I don't want this to be a one-time catch up kind of thing. I meant it when I said I don't want there to be a time when you're not a part of my life again. I don't think I would survive it twice. I still love you, Valencia and that has never changed."

She turned to him after he closed the trunk.

"Ethan, I had a wonderful time tonight and like you, I don't want what has happened between us to end either. I agree we need to talk, but let's do it after we've both had some sleep. I'm hoping Lina will sleep in at least for another two hours."

Ethan laughed. "I would apologize for not letting you sleep, but only two of those additional times were my fault. The others were yours when I thought I was dreaming about where your mouth was until I woke up and looked down to see it wasn't a dream. No way was I going to be able to deny you that or me for that fact," he said smiling like a sly cat who had been up to no good.

"I guess we couldn't get enough of each other," she said.

"I know that I never will, but the ball is in your court with where we go from here. I want to be all in, no doubt. You think about it and let me know what you decide, okay?"

"I will, but I already know that I am all in, too, but let's talk more later."

"Tell your sister and brother-in-law I said hello. I'll be in town for a few more days and then I'm flying out to Baltimore to watch my brother's game. I'd like to see you before I go and it's a given that I want to see you when I return."

"Why don't you come by tomorrow if you have time and meet Marco and the kids? My sister will also be here late in the afternoon."

"I have all the time in the world for you. I have a photoshoot in the morning, but I should be done around three. Is that good?" he asked as they walked to the door.

"That's perfect. I'll pick up some stuff we can cook on the grill and enjoy some time talking. I have no doubt Marco will have a million questions for you on top of the grilling my sister will give you. As you know, she is never at a loss for words."

"Yes, I remember her very well. I have a busy day of meetings today, but I will call you later this evening. What can I bring tomorrow?" he asked.

"Yourself, that's all you need to bring."

"Come on, I can't show up empty handed. Why don't I stop and pick up some more desserts from the restaurant?" he asked, knowing how much she loved the pie.

"Okay, but that's it. Don't you show up with a car load of food – I have it covered," she said.

"You got it, now go ahead inside and I'll talk to you later."

Valencia turned to unlock the door and stopped.

"Promise me you won't blow this up with your father later today. I know you still plan to talk to him. If we're going to make a go at this, we have to let go of the past hurt and we can't do that if it blows up now, nine years later. Don't let this ruin anything going forward."

Ethan knew he had no intentions of letting anything ruin the high he was currently on.

"I promise, I won't. I am going to talk to him, but I'm going to vent and let him know how disappointed I am to hear what he did, but then I promise you, I will hug him and let it go. He needs to know that I know, okay?"

Ethan knew there were some things that can't be dismissed as if they never happened.

"Thank you. Be safe driving home," Valencia said right before she closed and locked the door. She assumed everyone was still asleep since it was very early in the morning. After activating the alarm, she watched him through the front window as he hopped in his car and drove away.

Turning around, she was startled to see Aimee standing on the steps leading upstairs looking at her.

"Have fun? I wasn't expecting you back until much later?" she asked.

"You scared me. Why are you lurking in the dark?"

"Girl, I'm not lurking. I heard the car when it pulled up and I've been waiting for an eternity for you to come inside. What was going on out there and what happened last night. Walk across the room and let me see if you're walking funny?"

Valencia had to put her hand over her mouth to keep from laughing loud enough to wake everyone else up.

"It's six in the morning and we were talking. You are crazy and I'm not walking funny."

"Did you have a good time?"

"I had the best time. It was magical and I can't tell you how special he made me feel."

"It's because he still loves you and I have a feeling that it's mutual. I'm not discounting anything about Harley, but that first love is always special. Noow that you've connected again, I can see it's not teenage love anymore. Am I right?"

Valencia walked over and sat down on the steps.

"Is it crazy that I have feelings for him after two days?"

"Val, it's been longer than two days. It's been over nine years of love that you never forgot about and you never let go of. There's nothing wrong with that. The fact that you found each other again and it seems the way you feel about each other is mutual, tells me things are working out the exact way they were meant to be and I'm glad. Why don't you get some sleep and when Lina gets up, I'll get her? I have a feeling you haven't had much sleep?"

Valencia walked past her up the stairs.

"I've been up all night and I feel euphoric."

"That's what good lovin' will do for you."

"I hope it's every single time," Valencia admitted.

"I have a feeling with the two of you, it will be. Good

night, sis."

Valencia smiled and waved.

"Good morning and good night."

Before going into her room, she peeped in on Lina who was sound asleep in Lucia's room. Closing the door, she went into her room and closed the door behind her. Now that she was home, she was finally getting sleepy. Though her body was tired from the workout Ethan had given her all night long, her mind was still on a high after the night they'd had. There was something to say for a man who no longer made love like a teenage boy. Back then, he was her first and she had experienced many firsts with him and some were even firsts for him, but tonight he made love to her like no experience she'd ever had. The way he touched her, kissed her, caressed her and made her body come alive, she could have stayed in bed with him all day. She had been as insatiable for him as he was for her. As she removed her clothes and grabbed pajamas, her body was still sensitive in the area between her legs where his length and very thick width had her screaming in delight all night long. Memories of the night in his bed and then the early morning shower together had her body still tingling, remembering him.

Just as she climbed into bed, her cell phone pinged. She smiled knowing it was probably Ethan letting her know he was home. She read his text.

'Just pulling into the garage and I was thinking about you. I had a great time and I can't wait to see you again. Get some rest. You wore a brother out and

I'm planning to catch a nap for a few hours before visiting my parents and heading to my meetings. See what you do to me? I need more rest after you than I do after a game. I meant it when I said I loved you. I'll call you later. Sweet dreams.'

Valencia had so much she wanted to say and it was more than she wanted to put in a text. She decided to send a quick, short message that she hoped said everything that he needed to know.

'I love you, too.'

And she really did. Turning over in bed, sleep finally captured her in its grasp.

Sixteen

Ethan woke to the sound of his ringing phone. He hadn't been asleep that long, though sunlight poured through his bedroom window. After dropping Valencia off at home, he was on a high that nothing could bring him down from. He tossed once he got in bed, not able to escape the thoughts of the night with her. He could still smell her scent on the pillow and all over his sheets.

After finally getting to sleep, he wasn't happy that someone couldn't wait until a better hour of the day to call him. Blindly reaching for his phone, he answered.

"This had better be an emergency," he said loudly.

"I'm your brother and I don't need an emergency to call you. Why are you still in bed? I expected you to be up working out, which is your usual routine," Eli said.

"E, do you know what time it is?" he asked, closing his eyes and rolling back over.

"Yes. It's a time when you're never in bed this late.

What gives? You sick or was it a woman? It must have been a woman. Is she still there and did I interrupt something? That's not sleep I hear in your voice?" he quipped.

"E, really?" Ethan slurred out.

"I'm just saying. I'm still trying to be like you with a woman in every city. Are you back in Miami yet?"

"Yeah, I've been here a few days. I was going to call you later to tell you I'm still coming to Baltimore for your game. I think this is a double-header? If so, I'm staying for both."

"Man, I can't wait to see you. We haven't had time to celebrate your win for the season."

Ethan knew it was a ritual for him and Eli to get together at the end of their respective seasons and celebrate, win or lose.

"The way you've been playing, I would say your team is in good standing for a championship win this season, though it's still pretty early."

"Yeah, we're doing something. You still didn't answer my question about why you're still in bed? You took Aubrey with you to Miami?" Eli asked.

Ethan heard her name and it didn't give him the happy feeling Valencia's name gave him.

"No, I didn't."

"I didn't think so and I don't even know why I asked. I knew that wasn't going to last. She was all about the fame – an educated groupie," he snickered.

Ethan laughed. He and Eli had many conversations about the fact that Aubrey was a very intelligent woman with a post-graduate degree, but that didn't keep her from acting like a silly, immature groupie from time to time. She was good company when Ethan needed it, but he knew it would never amount to much.

"You're funny. It wasn't Aubrey, it was Valencia," he admitted and waited for the storm to hit when Eli made the connection. The shock factor would stun him and it made him smirk on his end of the phone.

"Wait, who? Did you say Valencia as in Valencia Ramos that you dated back in high school? What the hell? How did that happen? I haven't heard you say her name in years? When did you reconnect with her?"

Ethan laughed hearing Eli babble like an excited child on the other end.

"When I returned to Miami. I ran into her at a baseball game and we reconnected."

"Damn! That's major. What was that, a roll in the sack or something more?"

Ethan sat straight up in bed.

"Bro, she has never been that for me and you know it. I'm still in love with her."

"Wow, that's huge. You and your first love back together again. I don't believe it. Have you told mom and pop? What about Esha? Does she know?" he asked.

Ethan was ready for them all to know about it, but not at this ungodly hour.

"Look, I will answer every question you have, but can it wait until later?" Ethan asked, yawning.

"I got you. I was calling to remind you about my game, but you already remembered. I see we'll have a lot to catch up on when you get to Baltimore. I'll see you in a few days. I'm glad about Valencia. I know what she means to you and has meant all these years. I want the full story when you get here."

"Later, E," Ethan said, not waiting for a response before hanging up. As sleep took him in, he smiled as the last thought on his mind turned to Valencia.

~~

"Hey sis, you alright today?"

Valencia opened her eyes slightly and looked into Aimee's smiling face as she plopped down on the other side of the bed. Feeling the sunlight from the window on her face, she tried to fight the fact that it was morning already.

Looking around the room through one eye, she expected to see and hear Lina.

"Where's Lina and how long have I been asleep?" she asked, groggy from not enough sleep.

"I was going to take them out for breakfast, but for some reason everybody overslept. I made them waffles and they're downstairs with Marco. He's leaving for work in about ten minutes. I didn't want to wake you up, but I didn't know if you really wanted to sleep the whole day away or if you wanted to venture with us to the park."

"Oh, I'm glad you woke me. I want to go with you to the park and then see if you're open for a cookout tomorrow. I know it'll be Sunday, but Ethan and I talked about him coming over and meeting Marco and the kids and I already told him it was a good idea. I hope that was okay knowing I should have checked with you first."

"What! Really? He's coming over here to our house for a barbecue? Marco is going to die!" Aimee screamed, jumped up and danced around the room.

"Nothing big Aimee."

"So, the two of you are going to keep this thing going? It wasn't just a booty call?"

Valencia sat up in bed and winced when she moved.

"No, it wasn't a booty call."

"Damn, it must have been something if you're aching like that. You can barely move. He put it on you, huh?" Aimee laughed.

Valencia laughed along with her.

"I had no idea I would be this sore. It was a pretty passionate night and every ache I'm experiencing was well worth it. I haven't been with anyone since Harley and that was months before he passed because he was away. He had just arrived home when the accident occurred. We were planning a sexy night that night when the accident happened. I guess my body wasn't use to that kind of workout, but oh, was it incredible. Ethan is the kind of stuff that sexy movies are made about. I need to get a good soak in the bathtub. Can you bring Lina up and I'll bathe her with me? What time are we going to the park?"

"Well, it's just about eleven in the morning now. We'll go around one."

"Okay, that works for me. I'll be up and dressed by then."

"Are the two of you officially dating now or what is this?"

Valencia wasn't sure, but she knew it was the start of something wonderful.

"I think we are. We didn't really talk about it last night because we were busy, but in the drive home this morning, he wants to spend time together and he made it very clear last night was not reliving some boyhood dream of getting back in my panties. We came to the realization that what we felt back then was real and the reasons behind our breakup had nothing to do with us."

"What does that mean? You never told me what happened. You've always kept that to yourself, though I had a feeling it had something to do with our father. He mumbled something back then, but he didn't make any sense."

Valencia exhaled. "Have a seat for a minute."

"I think Ethan's father paid our father to break Ethan and I up. I don't know all of the details, but it took a lot of convincing on my part to keep Ethan from bringing his full rage down on his parents. He plans to talk to them, but I think his rage isn't as out of control as it was last night. What he and I thought occurred all these years, isn't how it happened when we shared the story from our different perspectives. It came down to Ethan's father being responsible and he was mad. I mean he was really mad. When we got to his condo, which was amazing I must say, we talked a little and he was fuming. I don't think he needs to say anything to them, but Ethan thinks differently. I'm going to let him handle this however he sees fit. If he and I are going to date, we can't have that holding over us. He's close with his family and we can't avoid them. I only hope it doesn't blow up worse and that Ethan has been able to calm down."

"Wow. When is he planning to talk to his father?"

"Today. I'll find out what happens when I talk to him later."

"What about when he returns to Denver for the season? What happens between the two of you then?"

Valencia sat up on the edge of the bed.

"All I can answer for is right now. Ethan and I will have to deal with that when the time comes. Now, what about today?" Valencia stood slowly knowing she was sore from their enthusiastic night of lovemaking, but moving should help until she gets in the tub.

"We have food to buy after the park because you can't have old run of the mill stuff for a star. They are used to everything being top of the line."

"Aimee, we're not going out of our way. I know we see the five-star treatment being given to the elite in society, but Ethan is not like that. He's rich and can buy the top of the line of whatever he wants. I think what he wants most is just an evening of fun. Let's get some board games, card games, invite a few of Marco's friends from work and their wives and husbands. Call Rosita and let's get regular food and drinks and just have a good time. I want him to get to know you and Marco and to meet Lina."

Aimee faked pouting.

"Okay," she dragged out.

"Let's get the kids dressed and then do a little shopping and let Marco get to the dealership and work on who he wants to invite. Please tell him not to mention Ethan? The world knows who he is and I don't want people hiding in bushes trying to capture pictures of him. They will see it's him when they get here," Valencia pleaded.

"Okay, that works. I'll go down and keep an eye on the kids, so that he can get going while we wait for you to shower and dress. I've already bathed them all. I will put their clothes on."

Seventeen

After spending an incredible night with Valencia, Ethan finally got his mind together to deal with his father. Even though she asked him to let it go, he couldn't. He did promise her that he would approach him with a level head and he would. He needed answers and he was planning on getting them today.

Now fully awake after grabbing breakfast and a quick workout in the gym he'd converted one of the bedrooms too, he pulled his car out of the garage and drove in the direction of his parent's house.

He had a lot on his mind he wanted to say and rehearsed it several times to be sure it was toned down. He couldn't get over the fact that for nine years, his father held a secret from him, knowing what losing Valencia had done to him. Sure, he went on to do great things in his career, but his private life was never the same again.

He thought back to the eighteen-year-old Ethan he

was then and remembered how he'd shocked himself with how fast he'd fallen for Valencia. Over ice cream, he'd fallen in love and knew it the moment it happened. No one understood how deeply he felt for her back then; only he and Valencia knew. Now, to find that his father had a hand in what happened to their love, he was having a hard time taking the idea in. What could he have been thinking? Did he do what he did all for a career in professional basketball for his son? Did he want that more for him than to see him happy? What parent does that? He knew it wasn't rare, but he didn't expect it from his own father. He used money to ruin what he and Valencia had. If it wasn't for Valencia asking him to tread lightly, he would really lay his feelings out on the line for his father, but he'd made her a promise. She was correct that if they planned to have any type of relationship going forward, he had to get beyond this and not harbor any ill-will.

Ethan thought about the wasted years and the fact that Valencia had gotten married and had a child. He was glad that she'd met a great guy who loved her, but he couldn't help, but feel a little jealous. He was the one who was supposed to make her happy and give her the children she always said she wanted. He was happy for her that her life had been a good one and that she hadn't been stuck in the life that she had lived back then that she hated. Valencia always wanted to get out and make something of herself and he was elated that she had done that. Now is their time and he wouldn't jeopardize a second chance with her for anything. He would say what he needed to say and then make peace with it and move on.

As he continued driving, he dialed his parent's house hoping to catch his father in. He knew he had a tendency to get an early start, but hoped today wasn't one of those days.

"Hey, Mom, is Pop at home or did he leave for the office already?" he said the moment she answered.

Moriah heard something different in Ethan's voice and knew why he was calling.

"He's here. He's off for a few days. With a lot of contract signings taking place after the draft with his long list of new clients, he's getting a few days of relaxation in before diving in. I'm sure he anticipates a lot of late evenings coming up soon. Is everything okay? Your voice sounds a little strange," she said, already knowing the answer, but hoped she could get more out of him before she connected him with Tellis. She was the peacekeeper in the family and she had a feeling that skill would be needed today. A mother's intuition was telling her that those old chickens that they thought were dead and buried were suddenly alive and well and on their way home to roost.

"I'm fine. I just need to talk to Pop. I'll be pulling up to the house in a few minutes. Let him know I'm coming and I'd like to talk to him if he has the time."

"He always has the time for you kids. I'll let him know. See you soon," he said and hung up.

Standing from her comfortable place at the kitchen counter, Moriah went in search of her husband to warn him about the storm that was brewing and about to visit them. She found him in his office just hanging up from a call.

"You're up early," Tellis said the moment she entered. "I thought you were planning to sleep in late today which is why I came down here to the office to do a few things until you got up. I was hoping we could get a game of tennis in today," he said.

"I know. I ended up having an early phone call with a client and was supposed to have another one in about an hour, but now I'm going to postpone it in case you need me here at home."

Tellis looked at her confused.

"I don't think I will unless there is something I forgot that I needed to do. Besides the game of tennis, my day should be quiet."

"I'm not so sure you're going to have that kind of day. Ethan is on his way here to talk to you."

Tellis looked up at her with a blank stare on his face.

"He is?" he asked.

"Yes, he is and I have a feeling it's about Valencia. Remember I told you they were having dinner last night. There's a good chance they talked about what happened when they were kids and they probably know that things didn't happen the way they each thought. The sound in Ethan's voice wasn't the same. I'm going to hang around to help keep some control. You remember how much he loved that girl and if he knows what you did, knowing it resulted in him losing her, I have a feeling this isn't going to just blow over. Ethan is normally the calmest and most laid back of our kids, but he's never been confronted with anything the likes of his own father paying someone to keep a girl he was head over heels in love with away from him."

Tellis exhaled, frustrated at himself at the remembrance of what he'd done.

"You know why I did it. I know it was wrong and if I could take it back, I would do it in a minute, but I can't," he confessed.

"Why you did it won't matter. You didn't hear him talking about her yesterday. He's still in love with her and as his mother and knowing my children the way I do, it's why he has never been able to commit to a woman beyond anything casual. There has always been something missing in his life all these years that money and fame were unable to fill. He is one of the highest paid athletes in the world and can have anything he wants and yesterday I realized the one thing he truly wants is Valencia and he always has."

"Love, I can apologize until I have no more words to say and it won't help what happened back then. I will let him say his peace and ask for his forgiveness. He's still young and if they are still in love with each other, there is time for them to have that love. I know it doesn't equal to them sharing that love since they were eighteen years old, but it's something."

Moriah paused. "You should have told him by now."

Tellis no longer made eye contact with her and she knew he was feeling bad enough about the situation. She didn't need to make it worse by badgering him about something he couldn't fix. Before he could reply, they heard Ethan calling out for them as he entered the house.

"We're in your father's office," Moriah said, loud enough for him to hear them.

"Let me talk to him alone," Tellis said before Ethan stepped into the office.

"Respect his hurt, Tellis. Respect it and own up to your part," she said.

"I will, my love," he said and smiled.

"Hey guys," Ethan said coming into the office.

"Hi. You're out extra early this morning," Moriah said.

"I have a photoshoot and meetings today," he said.

"I have a client meeting this morning. I'll leave you and your father to talk unless you need to speak to us together," she inquired.

Moriah struggled with wanting and not wanting to stay. She loved her kids more than anything and she would always want to push their hurt away, but this time, she knew Ethan needed to work this out with his father.

Ethan looked between them, "No, I just need to talk to Pop."

Moriah gave Tellis one last look of love and support knowing that this was going to be a hard conversation and she left, closing the office door behind her.

Ethan turned to his father trying his best to hold on to his pleasant demeanor.

"A day of golf today? Mom said you were taking a

few days off."

Ethan wasn't sure how to lead into the conversation and so that he presence didn't seem intimidating in any way just in case his anger raged he took a seat in one of the leather recliners facing his father's desk.

"We have a lot of new contracts being signed and I wanted a few days' break before the late nights in the office. Your mother said you had something to talk to me about? We need to talk about your new contract and a few other offers that have been coming in for endorsements for. I do get the feeling that work isn't what you want to talk about."

Tellis didn't want to drag the moment out if in fact Ethan came to talk about Valencia.

"I do. Did mom tell you who I ran into the other day?"

"You mean Valencia Ramos? Yes, she told me. I hope she's well."

Ethan paused. "Do you?" he asked in an even tone. He never raised his voice to his father and even though his anger was building up again, he never would.

"Do I what?" Tellis asked.

"Do you hope she's well?"

Tellis paused and from the look on Ethan's face, he was holding back on what he really wanted to say.

"You know, I'll assume this is about what I did nine years ago?" Tellis asked.

"You did it? You gave her father money to keep her away from me?" Ethan said, raising his voice a little.

"I did and there hasn't been one day that I haven't

regretted it. Once it was done, I couldn't take it back."

"You could have told me about it and I could have fixed it. How could you even do that to begin with? Do you have any idea what you took from me? What you took from us both?"

Ethan continued to speak with a calm voice because despite the anger he felt, this was his father, the man who had guided his career and helped him get to where he was in life. He also recognized that this was also the man who played a dangerous game with his son's heart and loss.

"I thought it was puppy love and you were on the precipice of a future that most kids your age only dream about. All I saw was you wasting your time focused on a girl."

"It wasn't puppy love, Pop."

"Ethan, I know that now and I've known it as the years went by. Believe me, your mother reminded me often that something in you was missing."

"Mom knew about this?"

"She only knew after it was done. Over the years on many occasions, she encouraged me to talk to you about what I did. I contemplated it a few times, but then time got away as your career took off and there was one major achievement after the other. You were dating and involved with other women and I just let it go. I know there are no words to offer you that would make you feel any better or change what I've done, but I am sorry. I am truly sorry for what I've done to you and Valencia. If she would allow me the opportunity, I would like to apologize to her face to face."

Ethan wanted to be mad, but he couldn't be mad at his father, he only had one and his sincerity in his apology told him that it was a horrible thing he'd done, but then Valencia's words stuck with him. She was right that they were where they are right now and that means he has another chance with his first love. Carrying around anger wasn't going to help the situation.

"I came here angry at you Pop after finding out what you did and making Valencia think she wasn't good enough for me. I loved her unconditionally. She didn't have to be a particular kind of girl or have dreams bigger than the eye could see. She didn't have to come from a certain class of family or have parents who walked around with their noses in the air. She loved me and that was all I needed from her then and it's all I need from her now. It wasn't puppy love – it was real love and she was my first love."

Tellis stood and walked around his desk so that they could speak closer.

"I know that love because I've loved your mother like that since my college ball playing years. I'm sorry I took that experience from you. Is there anything I can do to make this right?" he asked.

Tellis knew he never, ever wanted any of his children to not have the kind of love he had with his wife. Ethan learned early that money wasn't everything and he respected that his son loved from his heart and not from his wallet.

"You don't have to make anything right. I didn't come here for you to seek my forgiveness. I wanted to talk to you to let you know how your actions hurt Valencia and I and by some crazy fate, I reconnected with her after all of these years by spotting her in a crowd at the stadium. That was something I say was meant to be. There is no way I can be angry about that. Maybe back then, I wasn't ready to handle being in love and still follow the path that led me where I am today. I can tell you that I am still in love with her and I think she feels the same way. We plan to find out if we have something that we can actually make last this time and for that, I'm happy. I will take you up on your offer to apologize to her in person. She deserves that from you and I want the family to finally get to know her. You'll be seeing lots of her."

"Anything son and you're right – she deserves an apology from me."

Ethan stood and gave his father a hug.

"I love you, Pop and nothing could ever change that. I'm glad we've cleared the air."

"So am I. Do you have some time to tell me about her? I'd really like to know more about the woman who has had my son's heart since he was a boy."

Ethan laughed and grinned like that young boy in love with a beautiful young girl from the basketball court.

"I have a little time. Let's get some coffee while I let mom know she can go ahead and leave us alone. I sensed she knew what this was about and I doubt if she's left this house until she knows everything is good."

Tellis patted him on the back as they walked out of the office.

"You and your mom are two peas in a pod," Tellis quipped.

Eighteen

Ethan sat back and laughed with Marco and few of his friends who were invited over for the cookout. He hadn't had this much fun in a long time. A lot of times when he went to events, people wanted to be in his space because he was Ethan Bennett, star basketball player, but Valencia made sure that everyone first, knew who he was and then she made it clear that he was at the cookout to enjoy himself and to get to know her family, not for them to bombard him with questions about other players or about money and other things they should stay clear of. Thankfully, everyone abided by her wishes and he knew it was because they didn't want to suffer her wrath.

The best part of his evening was getting to know her daughter, Lina. She was a sweet little girl and she had him wrapped around her little finger from the moment she came over to him and handed him several of her dolls. When he started playing with her dolls with her and sat on the grass with her, they were inseparable for the remainder of the evening. When it was time for Valencia to put her to bed, she walked over to him like it was the most natural thing to do and grabbed his hand to take him with her. Everyone laughed at how serious Lina was about him going with her.

He walked with Valencia inside the house and would slip away when she gave her a bath and put her in bed. Valencia called him back in when Lina wanted to say goodnight. He was a goner the minute her little arms circled around his neck. That was a reminder of what was missing from his life. It wasn't just Valencia that was missing after all those years, but it was the dream of the family they were supposed to have together.

As the night was coming to a close and people began to leave, he stuck around to help Valencia, her sister and Marco clean up. Since Aimee and Marco did most of the setup, Valencia sent them off to their room and the two of them focused on the rest of the cleanup duties.

"I had a fun time. It felt good to sit back and relax and that pasta salad you made was delicious. I hope you saved me some to take home."

"I saw how empty your refrigerator at the condo was and I put several containers of food away for you to take back with you."

He leaned down and kissed her.

"I haven't had a chance to buy much food and I thank you for taking notice that a brother needs to eat," he laughed while loading the dish washer.

"I'm glad you came over tonight. My family loved you and I don't know what to say about little miss Lina. I haven't seen her laugh that much in a very long time. I think her favorite thing was you riding her around on your shoulders and playing with her dollies. She gets frustrated with me when it comes to playing with dolls because I don't think I do it the way she wants. You seem to have perfected it right away."

Ethan came up behind her and pulled her back flush against his body while placing his head down on her shoulder.

"Your daughter bought and sold me hook, line and sinker tonight. I enjoyed entertaining her as much as she enjoyed entertaining me. I do have to learn all of those songs she likes to sing if I'm going to be hanging around. She didn't like that I didn't know all of the nursery rhymes the two of you sing."

Valencia turned around in his arms.

"You know I want you hanging around, right? I know we haven't had our talk, but I don't want you leaving here tonight not knowing how I feel. I wasn't expecting any of this and I certainly didn't expect that I would still be in love with you too, but I am. I love you very much, Ethan Bennett. Nothing would make me happier than to see what's next for us, if you still want that."

Ethan didn't speak. His attention was focused on her face and on her lips as she uttered the words he never thought he'd hear again; she still loved him, too. He remembered her text, but it didn't match hearing the words come from her mouth. That was all he needed to hear and all he wanted out of life. He would give up everything he had achieved if it meant he would have her back where she was always meant to be.

He answered in a way that left no doubt about what his intentions were. His heart skipped a beat, knowing that he was going to get a second chance at a love that he'd never let go of. Deep down, he knew that is was because of the lack of closure to their past that kept him from a future with anyone else. He'd never forgotten about his first love and to be standing with her in his arms was more than just a dream come true; it was his life finally being back on track.

His eyes met hers and he took in everything about her from the way her hair flowed down around her shoulders to the gleam in her light brown eyes. He even smiled at the perfect shape of her nose. She was his again and he would never let her go again.

Ethan lowered his head. "I love you," he said.

"I love you, too," Valencia replied.

Ethan didn't want anything else at the moment except to feel the soft caress of her lips against his.

He kissed her soft and sweetly at first and when she embraced him and his openmouthed kiss, he shut out everything except for the way she tasted. This was life to him, he thought.

They were swept away in the feeling of knowing that this kiss was a new beginning for them to indulge in their first love again. As they pulled away, he knew that his body was calling for a repeat of the night before, but he didn't want to take her away from Lina again.

"Spend the night with me," Valencia said, catching him off-guard.

"Where? Here at your sister's house?" he asked, remembering their night before and how ardent they were for each other.

"Yes, here. There is a spare bedroom on the back of the house, beyond the family room where I was originally going to sleep, but then I decided to put Lina in the room with Aimee's daughter Lucia and I didn't want to be on a different level if she woke up and didn't see me close by. I want to feel you," she admitted.

"If you think it's okay, I would do anything for you."

His heart melted when she smiled up at him.

"Good, because all I want tonight, is you."

There was one subject he wanted to get out of the way.

"I want to talk to you about one thing because it involves some of your time tomorrow."

"What is it?"

"I talked with my father yesterday and in the beginning, I thought it would be a shouting match, but that didn't happen. He was prepared for the discussion and I think he'd been prepared for it for a lot of years. He was very apologetic and he had no idea that what we felt for each other back then was real, even though he and my mother fell in love around the same age. I accepted his apology, but what he really wants is to apologize to you in person for what he did. I want to take you by the house to see my parents and let him say what he needs to say. You don't have to do this if you don't want to. I thought it would help clear the air of any awkwardness with us dating. I meant it when I said I don't have any plans of you not being in my life for the foreseeable present and future."

"Will it mean that much to you?" she asked.

"Yes, it would because until we clear up the past, I think it will hang over our future and I don't want that. I love you and if my future is going to be with you and Lina, let him apologize and explain if he feels the need to. You can either accept it or not accept it. I do agree that he owes it to you just as he owed it to me."

"I'm fine with that. Though it will have no impact on our future because I think we've both realized we don't ever want to be apart again, I agree he owes us both an apology for the years we've been apart because of his scheme, but I won't look down on the full past."

"I don't want you to do that. For starters, there is Lina and as much as I know she is the love of your life, she already means the world to me and we can never discount that part of your life. We can't move on and have this thing hanging around like a sore thumb."

"I agree and I look forward to it."

"Good. Now, what about this secret room where no one can hear you scream my name," he said slyly.

Valencia laughed and took his hand to lead the way. After turning out the light and setting the alarm, they hurried toward more of what they shared the night before.

"This house is much bigger than it looks from the

outside."

"I said the same thing the first time I saw it. There are four bedrooms and three bathrooms upstairs and this bedroom here has its own bathroom. There's also the powder room that everyone used today during the cookout. How big is the house you have?" she asked, entering the room and closing the door.

"It's pretty big, too big for just me, but it's my getaway place when I want to be close to home, but not close enough for people to pop up unannounced. It has seven bedrooms total and eight bathrooms. As with most players, I have a basketball court outside and one indoors. There are two pools and lots of space for us to have some fun. I'll take you to see it after I come back from Baltimore visiting with my brother."

Valencia watched Ethan as he walked around the room checking everything out. Little did he know that she was spending her time checking him out as she began removing her clothes. She moved quicker when he walked into the adjoining bathroom.

"I can't wait to see it," she said, while she removed her shorts, tank top. Just as he re-entered the room from the bathroom, she had removed the last of her clothing and was bent over with her backside in his direction as she slid her panties down her legs.

"Damn!" Ethan said a little louder than he'd planned, forgetting for a second where they were. All he could think about was her luscious behind and its invitation to him.

Valencia stood and turned around, placing her

hands on her hips.

"You like?" she asked, purring like a cat.

"I love and you know it," he said, quickly divesting himself of his own clothing.

Valencia stopped smiling and paused.

"Shoot, do you have any condoms? I don't have any and I'm not on any kind of birth control. I know my timing sucks considering I'm already standing here naked and in a few seconds, so will you. We can always do some other things, if not."

Ethan reached for his wallet in his shorts he'd already thrown to the floor in his excitement at seeing her naked and ready for him.

"I put two in my wallet not knowing when the mood would strike us. I want to be sure we don't have any hindrances when it comes to making love whenever and wherever we want," he said grinning when he retrieved the two condoms.

"I guess we'll have to make due with two since I know we used four or five of them last night. I guess I'll have to let you sleep some," she said.

Valencia walked over to him and took the condoms from his hand.

"I'm not thinking about sleep right now in case you haven't noticed," he said pointing to his erection which was pointed directly at her.

"That's good to know. Let me hold on to this one for now because I have something else in mind."

Valencia gave Ethan a little push and he fell back onto the bed, laughing out loud.

"I love a woman who takes charge," he said.

Coming up over him as the air tingled with her desire to have him. She quickly kissed his lips before kissing a path down his hard, muscled chest and followed the thin path of hair that led to that part of him that brought her pleasure over and over and over again. She more than craved him again even as her body quivered at the remembrance of the night before.

"Your body is beautiful, like a perfect work of art. I love everything about it," she said.

"I know what you have in mind. I barely survived when you did it last night. I thought I was going to die right on the spot if it's possible to do from feeling so good."

He started to say more, but words flew out of his mouth the moment her mouth covered the large head of him. His head began to spin as she made love to him with her mouth licking, sucking and tasting him, driving him made with desire. Ethan had to remember where they were though he felt like he could roar like a lion.

He looked down at her as she looked up at him. The look he saw on her face was pure love; love for him and love for how she was loving him. When he was on the brink, he knew he wanted to be inside of her.

"Come here, baby," he said and pulled her up, kissing her passionately. "I need to be inside of you right now. Your mouth felt so good, I'm not sure I would have lasted much longer and my pleasure is all about your pleasure."

"Your heart and how much you care is why I've always loved you," Valencia said, removing the condom from the wrapper and taking her time rolling it down his hardened flesh.

Straddling his body, she positioned herself to take him in and kept her eyes on his as she joined their bodies. She'd never had an appetite for love making the way she was developing with him. It was if he was an addiction she wasn't ready to give up.

She held onto his arms as Ethan held onto her hips, guiding their movement. As the pace quickened, so did her breathing. When she felt that all too familiar feeling soaring through every part of her body, she knew her release wasn't far away. The feeling was joyous as she clinched her toes as her body was beset with one torrential downpour of pleasure after another. Her body let go as her orgasm took her to unimaginable heights, reached only one other time in her life and that was the other night, still only with Ethan.

She moaned his name as she felt his body quake under hers while he moaned her name in return. She missed her Ethan and she said a quiet thanks that she had him back in her life again.

Nineteen

Valencia tiptoed into the kitchen to make her way upstairs to check on Lina. After making love twice in the night, she'd fallen asleep in Ethan's arms and delighted when she woke cocooned in his embrace. The hour was early with the sun just coming up over the horizon and she knew Lina would be up soon. Ethan was still sleeping and she didn't want to wake him.

"Why is it that I keep coming across my sister tiptoeing through the house," Aimee said humorously.

"That's because you're nosey, sis. Are the kids up?"

"Not yet, but it's almost time for them to get up. Is Ethan still here? I noticed you didn't sleep upstairs last night."

"Yes. He's in the guest room still sleeping. I was going to check on Lina to see if she was up yet. I hope it was okay that Ethan stayed the night."

"Girl, stop playing games. This is just as much your

house as it is mine and you can have anyone over here that you want, especially Ethan. You're in love and everyone could see it yesterday. Anytime he wants to come around to see you, he is always welcome. I want to see you get your life back and I can see that you're on the right path. It's only been a few days, but every time you say his name or I catch you thinking about him, you are lit up like a tree with bright lights. It makes me happy to see you happy."

Valencia sat down at the table as Aimee poured them both a cup of coffee. "I am happy. I haven't been this happy in a long time. I never thought I'd run into Ethan and definitely not be involved with him again.

"Mommy!"

Their heads turned toward the stairs and the sound of Lina calling.

"Sounds like Lina's up looking for me. Let me get her," Valencia said.

"I'm really glad you're here. I know I've said that a few times already, but life wasn't the same without you. I feel like we're whole again," Aimee said.

Valencia thought about her father and realized they weren't as whole as they should be. She was going to Ethan's parents' house in a few hours where his father was going to apologize for his actions. She already knew she was going to accept his apology because she loved Ethan and wanted a life with him. She also knew, if she could forgive someone else's father, she had to forgive her own.

"We're not as whole as we should be, but we'll get

there," she said.

Aimee looked at her questionably before figuring out what she meant.

"You're talking about Dad."

"I am. I'm going with Ethan to his parents' house today and the things his father did to put us on a path that separated us will soon be far behind us. I want to move on and have a happy, healthy relationship with him. If I can do that with his family in spite of what his father did, I can do that with my father. Do you know how to reach him?" she asked.

"I do."

"Give me a few days and then I want you to take me to see him. I don't know how it will go, but I need him to know that I know what he did and that it's old news. If we can build from that and he's clean from drinking and doing drugs, we're family and that includes all of us. I know that you've built some semblance of a relationship with him and I'm proud of you for doing that. I'm willing to try if he is."

Aimee tried to stop the tears from falling, but she couldn't. For years, she'd wanted her family back intact and they were getting closer to that. She stood and hugged Valencia, happy that they were a family again.

"I love you, sis."

"I love you, too, Aimee."

"Mommy!" Lina screamed again.

"Let me get her before she wakes up the entire house. I know I've said this a million times and I'm going to say it again – I'm happy to be home."

"We're all happy to have you back here with us.

~ ~

"Are you ready?" Ethan asked the minute they pulled up to the gate that led to his parents' house.

"I am." Valencia turned to Lina who was seated in the back in her car seat talking to her dolls a mile a minute. "Looks like she's ready, too. Are you sure about bringing her with us? Do your parents know that I have a daughter?" she asked as Ethan pushed in the security code to unlock the gate.

"Yes, they know and there is no better time like the present for them to be re-introduced to you and for them to meet Lina. We're in this together, right?" Ethan said.

"We're in this together."

Valencia sat back and relaxed as they drove up the winding road to the circle in front of the house. Ethan got out first and went around to the other side of the car to open her door and then to help Lina get out. He grabbed her bag and put all the dolls back inside just as he looked up and saw his mother standing at the front door.

"Hey, Mom!" Ethan said embracing her when he reached her.

"Ethan! I'm glad you're here." He watched as she then turned to Valencia. "It's good to see you, Valencia. You are still as beautiful as I remember you being. Who do we have here?" she asked looking at Lina.

"This is my daughter, Malina and we call her Lina."

Moriah leaned down to Lina's level.

"Hello, Lina. Look how pretty you are in your pink dress. It's nice to meet you," she said.

"Hello," Lina said and then grabbed onto Ethan's finger and Valencia's leg.

"Let's go inside. Your father is on a call and should be done shortly."

Ethan looked to Valencia to reassure her that everything was going to be okay. They entered behind his mother who escorted them into the living room.

"This room is beautiful," Valencia said looking around.

"Thank you. I recently had it redone. It's been redone a few times since the last time you were here. Why don't we sit and wait for Tellis? He should be right in."

"I'm here," Tellis said walking in behind them. "Son, Valencia, it's good to see you."

"Thank you, Mr. Bennett. Thank you for welcoming me into your home."

"And who do we have here?" he asked going down to Lina's level.

"This is Lina, my daughter. Say hello, Lina."

"Hello."

"Hello to you too. You look just like your mommy. Let's all have a seat," Tellis said standing to his full height and making his way over to sit next to Moriah on the sofa across from the chair where Ethan and Valencia sat. They all looked in wonder as Lina walked over and held her arms out for Tellis to pick her up. He lifted her up and placed her on the chair between him and Moriah. They all watched as she opened her little backpack and took out her dolls to play with.

Moriah spoke first. "So, Valencia, Ethan mentioned you lived in California? How was that?"

"It was wonderful. That move was my first time out of Florida. It was pretty foreign to me, but my husband made it bearable."

"We're sorry for your loss," Tellis said. "Ethan mentioned that he passed away."

"He did and thank you. He was a good man and loved Lina and I very much. We're happy to be back in Miami where I'm closer to my family and Lina gets to see the family."

"Family is important and one of the reasons I asked Ethan to bring you over was to apologize for not being the kind of family to Ethan that he should have had back then. One that was supportive of the decisions he made even at eighteen. One of those decisions was to fall in love with you and my apology extends to you, too. I know I can't take any of it back, but I hope you can forgive me enough to move on beyond this. It's obvious my son still loves you and I assume you feel the same way about him?" Tellis asked.

"Thank you and yes, I feel the same way about him. Once Ethan and I talked about what happened back then, we realized it was best to move forward and not harvest anger over the past. I appreciate your apology and I accept it. I don't know where things will go with Ethan and I, but I would love to know that what we have includes all of you."

Valencia meant every word. She would never want to take back her time with Harley, but she was ready to move forward with Ethan.

"I'm glad to hear we can put this behind us. I know Ethan and his father talked about it and it meant everything to Tellis to be able to apologize to you in person for the hurt he caused you both back then. I can't speak for anyone else, but it's good to see the two of you together. Now, I've had a light lunch prepared for us. I'm going to go see if there is anything else that needs to be done," Moriah said, standing.

"I'm going to go into my office and cut the computer and television off. When I heard you come in, I left everything on," Tellis said and stood. The minute he stood up, Lina hopped down from her spot on the chair, grabbed her dolls and started to follow him.

"I think I'll help you in the kitchen," Valencia said. "Come on with Mommy, Lina." When she reached for Lina's hand, Lina raced to keep up with Tellis as he turned to see that he was being followed.

"Well, it seems she prefers my company. Go ahead with Moriah and I'll keep an eye on her, I promise," he said.

"Pop?" Ethan started to question him.

"What? I may not have any grandchildren, but I have three children who were once this small and I still remember how to look after one. You survived!" he joked.

"If you sure you don't mind. It looks like she's not paying much attention to me," Valencia said.

"It's fine. Go ahead and I'll bring her in with me."

Tellis reached down and picked Lina up and carried her with him. Ethan smiled when he noticed the bright smile on Lina's face, a sign a child knows when they've gotten their way. It appears his father was next on the list of men that Lina will have wrapped around her finger before the end of the day.

~ ~

"What else did you have planned for the day?" Ethan asked as Valencia strapped a sleeping Lina into her car seat.

After spending the rest of the day enjoying his parent's company, they finally left when Lina fell asleep.

"I haven't thought much about it. I didn't have any plans other than relaxing with Lina. Would you like to join us in watching a few Disney movies?" she asked as they settled into the car.

"Well, I was thinking that you and Lina could join me in a relaxing evening at my place. I was hoping I could spend some time with the two of you before I left for Baltimore in another day. We could pick up a light dinner and whatever you need from the house and spend a quiet evening together; that is if you would like to."

"Are you sure?" she asked.

"I'm more than sure. Do I need to remind you again that we are a packaged deal, you, Lina and me? I'll take every chance I can get to stay in her good graces. She sure grew attached to my father today. She even called him Poppy."

"I know," Valencia said happily. "I asked him where did she get that from and he said he told her to call him Poppy and I swear she must have said it a hundred times during lunch."

"How did you feel about today?" he asked as they drove away from the house.

"Today was wonderful. Your parents made me feel very comfortable and the kind words from your Dad meant everything. I know he took full blame for what happened, but my father had a big role in that, too," she said.

As they drove through traffic, Ethan thought about the fact that the relationship between her and her father was still strained.

"Are you planning to talk to your father and try to work things out?"

"I am. Aimee and I talked about it this morning. I'm going to see him in a few days and talk some things out. It's time to finally heal my family."

"I'm happy to hear that because if we can bring what we had lost back together and hear my father take responsibility for what he did, anything is possible, including a relationship with your father. Now, about this evening – what do you think?"

"I think that's a great idea. Stop me by my sister's house and let me get Lina's folding crib and a few other things we'll need. We're all yours for the evening."

"I'm glad you agreed to go to that baseball game the other day with your sister. In a few short days, I am the happiest I have been in a lot of years and it's because of you. Maybe years ago, the timing wouldn't have been right for us, but it is now. I may not have appreciated what we had back then the way that I know I will appreciate it now. I could say I regret the time apart, but I don't because after all that's happened, I am loving the here and now," Ethan said.

"I couldn't agree more. It doesn't seem like it's only been three or four days since we ran into each other at the stadium. I came back to Florida without having any idea of how to really pick my life back up other than to focus on school and finding a job and now I feel much more complete with you."

"When do you finish school?"

"I'll be done by the time you head back to Denver for training. I'm hoping to dive into looking for a teaching job while Lina's in daycare every day. I'm hoping to sign her up in a few days."

"I want you to do whatever you want to do and if I can help in any way, let me know. We'll have to have a party to celebrate your graduation before I head to Denver."

Valencia smiled and looked out of the passenger window as they rode the rest of the way to her house in silence. For the first time, the word Denver rang out like a loud bell. Ethan would be returning to Denver to start the season soon and she knew how much she was going to miss him after they just got back together.

Ethan drove through traffic, sporadically looking over at Valencia who appeared to be deep in thought. If her thoughts matched his at all, he knew she was thinking about the fact that he would soon be leaving Florida to return to his life in Denver. He wondered what would happen to what was new and fresh for them. He would do anything to make sure they never drifted apart again. He hadn't figured out how to make that happen once he left Florida.

Twenty

"When is Ethan due back?" Aimee asked.

"Later today and I can't wait to see him. He went from Baltimore to visit Eli, then to Paris to visit Esha. He was going to come home in between those visits, but he didn't want to leave again until he has to fly to Denver. It seems like he's been gone forever and I miss him!"

"Right. He told me he wanted to do one trip and then get back to you and Lina," Aimee said.

"The day before he left, we took Lina to the zoo and to the beach, someplace she had never been. She didn't like the sand at first, but Ethan patiently worked with her until she realized it was something that wasn't going to hurt her. You should have seen her lift her little legs up every time he tried to put her feet in the sand. I think she didn't like the feeling of it between her toes. I took her the other day when you took Lucia to her doctor appointment and I had a time getting her to leave. This morning she said 'E' for Ethan. She still can't do the '*th*' sound yet, so she calls him 'E'. I let her facetime with him before putting her to bed last night and she was happy showing all the teeth she had in her mouth. They talked about dolls and puppies. She wants a puppy. Ethan would buy her a million puppies, but I told him to wait until I was in my own place before we address the puppy issue. It was fun watching them talk to each other, forgetting I was there," she laughed.

Valencia laid back further on the lounge chair on the deck in the back of the house with Aimee as the kids napped inside. She had been studying all day for her upcoming final exam with graduation looming. In a few hours, she and Lina were going to pack a bag and spend several days at Ethan's house. This was her first time getting a look at it since the first week they were together had pretty much been a whirlwind.

After having lunch with his parents and then spending the night at his condo watching movies until Lina fell asleep, they spent the night talking about what was next for them. They had avoided the biggest issue of him returning to Denver in a few weeks after her graduation, but they talked about how comfortably they'd fallen back in love.

"Make sure you call and tell me about this house of his. I know it's magnificent. I remember reading articles a few years ago when the house was being constructed. The layout I saw made the house seem enormous."

"He said he wanted to have everyone over before the

end of the summer for a big barbecue. You'll get to see it then or you can come out anytime over the next few days. Lina and I will be there."

"Girl, that man is coming back to spend time with his woman and that little girl in there and he does not want me and my brood intruding," Aimee said, turning over to let the sun evenly tan her skin.

"Nonsense," Valencia said dismissing the notion that Ethan would be against her coming out to the house.

"Things are going well with you two?"

"Yes, except he's a little pissed that the media has gotten wind of the fact that he's involved with someone from some leaked source. Before you get your panties in a bunch, he doesn't think it was anyone in our family. The day that he left for the airport and I dropped him off, he pretty much devoured me right in the drop-off area in the front of everyone standing there. People recognized him and then targeted me to find out who the woman was with him. The fact that he had security around him made our kiss stand out and cameras started flashing. He was more upset when I told him that there were cars following me from the airport. I called him from the car and he was about to turn around and come back out, but I told him I was fine. He told me to drive to the condo because the cars wouldn't be able to follow me there. I went and stayed in the condo for a few hours. Instead of driving my car back out, I called a car service and strangely enough, those cars were still waiting out on the street for me to come back out. They never saw me get in the car that pulled up."

"Is it going to be like that all the time? Is it safe for you and Lina?" Aimee asked concerned.

"It will be. Ethan and I talked about it and before long, paparazzi will be all over us. He's going to make sure no one bothers us and I'm sure it'll be fine."

"I'm happy for you. You should hear yourself when you talk about him. It's love, love, love!" Aimee proclaimed.

"It is love and I'm happy. Lina loves him, he loves us and right now, that's all I need." She was about to continue when her phone rang on the table beside her. Picking it up, she saw Ethan's name on the screen.

"Hey baby!" he said in her ear and she perked up.

"Hi. I miss you. Where are you? Are you stateside yet?" she asked.

"My jet just landed at the airport. I couldn't wait to get back to see you and Lina. Am I stealing you away from anything if I come pick you up on my way home?" he asked.

"No. We're already packed and ready. I can't wait to see you. How are Eli and Esha doing?" she asked.

"They're both good and looking forward to seeing you soon. I told them all about how we ran into each other and have been inseparable ever since. Esha can't wait to meet Lina. She'll be home in a few weeks around the time of your graduation. She's looking forward to seeing you again."

"I look forward to it. She was a young teenager the

last time I saw her. Now when I see pictures of the beautiful woman she has become, I don't recognize her. Imagine that – my boyfriend's sister is one of the top models in the world. I know people," she jibed.

"Yes, you do and because I know people, I was able to get us some tickets to Disney World in the hours before it opens for the public. There is a special day reserved for major league ball players and their families and I want to see if you want to take Lina and perhaps Aimee and Marco want to go with us and bring the kids. I know Lina loves Minnie Mouse and the princess. What do you think?"

Ethan was proud of himself. While he was away in Baltimore and in Paris, he couldn't think of anything but his two girls he had waiting for him in Florida.

"That sounds like fun. That's a good way to keep paparazzi and fans from swarming, preventing guys like you with families from enjoying the fun of the parks." She leaned over to Aimee. "Ethan has tickets to Disney on a day for professional players and their families. He wants to know if you and Marco want to come and bring the kids?"

Aimee almost fell out of her lounge chair. "Tell him yes! Are you kidding me? That means getting on rides with no lines? We are in!" she exclaimed.

Valencia turned back to her call. "I assume you heard that," she said to him.

"I did and good. I'm pulling out of the garage at the airport now and I'm heading to the condo to pick-up my car. I should be there to get you and Lina in about an hour. I hope you packed enough for more than just a few days."

Valencia smiled. She didn't want to wear out her welcome in Ethan's space, but it appeared he loved having them around as much as she loved being with him. "I'll pack a few more things. Do you mind if I give Aimee the address so that she and the family can visit?"

"Tell them they are welcomed anytime. As welcoming as they've been to me being at their house, of course they can come out anytime they want to."

"I will, but tonight, just me, you and Lina," she said.

"That's what I was hoping for. I missed my girls."

"We missed you, too."

"See you soon," Ethan said. "I love you."

"I love you, too, now get off the phone and come get us," Valencia laughed and stood up.

"I take it my future brother-in-law is on his way here."

Valencia stopped moving.

"What? No one said anything about marriage, so he is not your brother-in-law."

"Girl, that man knows what's good for him. He has waited nine long years to be with you and now that he is, you think he's going to wait forever to wife you? Think again. Thank me later when he pops the question."

Valencia waved her off and went inside the house to get Lina ready. She knew that whether Ethan ever proposed to her or not, she was happy. Lina woke up just as she reached for her, sprawled out on a blanket in the living room beside Lucia and Teemo who were still sleeping.

"You ready to go see Ethan?" she asked.

"E!" Lina exclaimed, stood and ran to the door.

"We have to change your clothes first and then we'll go.

"And a child shall lead them," Aimee said coming into the house. "She's knows that man will one day be her daddy."

"Oh, stop it," Valencia said, laughing as she made her was up the stairs.

~~

"Lina finally down?" Valencia asked.

"Yes, and it only took three stories this time. She fell asleep halfway through the second one, but kept bouncing up every time I stopped reading. That child of yours has strong will when it comes to not falling asleep," Ethan said entering the room.

When it was time for Lina to go to sleep, she only wanted him to read to her and he happily obliged.

"She thinks she's going to miss something. Did I thank you for setting up that room for her? She would have been comfortable in her travel crib."

"She had enough of that staying at the condo. While I was gone, I had a designer come in and add a few touches to one of the spare bedrooms. I wanted her to be more comfortable. I didn't do too much so that you would accuse me of spoiling her or going overboard. I want her to feel at home when she's here."

"Well, that room is definitely a plus in her column.

She was over the top excited when she saw it."

Valencia continued cleaning up the family room after their relaxing evening. Ethan had just returned to town and after picking them up, they opted for a night of catching up. After turning off the television thinking they were headed to the bedroom for a little private time, Ethan came up behind her and pulled her back against him, plowing her neck with one sexy open-mouthed kiss after another.

"You know how much I love when you do that," she said.

"All I thought about while I was gone was getting you back in my arms. Eli even accused me of not focusing on spending time with him because my mind was on you, which was partly true. I also had a few work things on my plate that I had to deal with. When I returned home, I didn't want any distractions for a few days. I wanted my time back home to be set aside for you and Lina. You haven't told me how the visit with your dad went."

"It went really well. We talked and I told him that you didn't have anything to do with what his father had done. I also told him that you and I were seeing each other again and that made him smile. We talked about my life over the years and he told me about his struggles. He's doing really good now. He lives with a woman, he's working and they actually have a nice place."

"When we have your graduation party, make sure you invite him. I'm glad you were able to repair your relationship."

"He loved Lina and she took to him good. Life has come full circle and that's a good thing."

"It is and now we can focus on us. With Lina down, it's time for some you and me time," he said smoothly and softly in her ear.

"Mmm, yes, it is. I've been ready for you since you left." Ethan's musk scent from his shower caused a trembling sensation that reached all the way to her stomach. She went into his arms as he picked her up and walked over to the couch, sitting down with her straddling his lap.

"I've missed this," he admitted before staring into her heated gaze. Her face showed a jaw-dropping sexiness that he knew he would never tire of seeing. He leaned forward and kissed her, making love to her mouth in a way that left no doubt about his love for her. As he deepened the kiss, he reached down and grasped her backside bringing her snug against that part of him that had already grown long and hard for her. He wanted her to feel how hard he was for her, displaying his strong need to be inside of her.

Valencia couldn't see as her vision blurred with a lustful haze. She couldn't think of anything except the way Ethan was making her body feel. Sensations traveled through her body and she was already feeling the embers that were stoking the fire that was setting her body up for an explosion of pure yearning. Time and time again, Ethan left her breathless and right now was no different. She moved a little as she sat astride him, feeling his powerful thighs between hers. She wanted him naked and the way he was reaching for her and removing her clothes, told her he was thinking the same thing.

They kissed and caressed almost impatiently as clothes flew to the floor. When she was left with only her shorts and panties on, Valencia threw her head back in wonder of whether she would be able to stand any more pleasure. Her desire for him was voracious as he teased her breasts with his mouth. He kissed them, nipped them, caressed them and then suckled them, driving her even more mad for him. She reached down to try and pull her shorts down, but was halted because of her current position across his lap. Hastily, she stood and quickly removed the last of her clothing before helping Ethan out of his.

Ethan looked at Valencia standing before him naked and before she knew what was happening, he growled and pulled her back onto his lap. The moment she was seated, his hands were everywhere, touching her, feeling her and familiarizing himself with every place that drove him crazy. He wanted to drag their pleasure out and knew that he had all night to do that – for now, he needed her, badly.

"I want this to last as long as possible, but I think I'm going to pass out if I don't get inside of you right now," he said, reaching for a condom he'd placed on the table after grabbing one from his room after putting Lina to bed. His hands were shaking so fiercely, he could barely get it open. He chuckled when Valencia took the pack from his hands and opened it.

"I got this, baby," she said and proceeded to cover his hard flesh.

Ethan tried to keep his eyes on her, but the feel of her hands on him made him throw his head back and close his eyes to keep from coming to an embarrassing end before satisfying her first.

"You're killing me, you know that right?" he asked through gritted teeth. "I think you know what you're doing to me and you're taking great pleasure in seeing me squirm. Well, I know how to make you squirm, too," he said.

Reaching between them, Ethan slipped his fingers over her already drenched opening and when he inserted a finger inside, he felt her hips wind in a circular motion and knew that she was already on the brink of exploding.

"Oh, that's not fair. I'm already close and I don't want to be. I want this to last at least to the point of feeling you inside of me. I'm not just talking about those long, delicious feeling fingers of yours," she said and kissed him the moment she had protection in place. Before she could rise and slide down over him, her body did explode as she tried to contain her screams of passion with Lina in the nearby bedroom.

To help stifle her sounds of pleasure, Ethan continued plunging her with his fingers as he covered her mouth with his lips allowing his body to engulf her sounds of delight at the work his fingers were putting in.

Needing to feel him, Valencia moved her body up and over his extremely hard, rigid penis and slid slowly down. Moving up and down on him in a swift motion, she felt like a rider on top of a powerful stallion, feeling free and wild taking control of their mutual satisfaction. The feeling of endless pleasure was almost unbearable as she rode him and he surged up into her with a powerful motion that was once again sending her to the edge of gratification.

Ethan felt it early, starting in his feet as he braced them on the floor to keep them from falling to the floor. As the intense feeling of letting go poured through him, he wanted her with him. He didn't want to take the ultimate ride without her.

"With me baby. I'm there and I need you with me," he whispered in her ear.

"I'm there," she uttered and then shattered in his arms as her orgasm slammed into her causing her to grind on him harder where the friction caused her orgasm to be prolonged into a never-ending abyss, a place she never wanted to be released from. Using the muscles between her legs, she gripped Ethan as he moved inside of her, calling her name over and over again. She felt his hot release as he used her neck to muffle his cries of pleasure. She held tight to him never wanting to let him go, ever again.

As her body went languid in his arms, Ethan laid them back on the chair, staying inside of her as their bodies calmed.

"You are my everything," he said.

"And you are mine."

Ethan reached for the blanket at the other end of the sofa, threw it over them as they drifted off to sleep.

Twenty-One

Ethan was on cloud nine as his family and Valencia's family gathered at his house outside of Miami to celebrate the completion of her online degree. He had two days left before he had to return to Denver to get ready for training for the upcoming basketball season. The past few months had been the best time of his life. In June, he hadn't set out to spend the entire summer in Florida, but that's what he did because of Valencia and Lina.

Looking around the room, he smiled at his brother and sister, thankful that they were able to move some plans around and join the family in celebrating Valencia knowing, how much it would mean to him.

With the remainder of the summer, he entertained Lina most evenings when he didn't have meetings or other appearances he had to make, allowing Valencia to focus on finishing her final assignments.

They spent most of their time either at his condo or at his house, where she and Lina had practically moved in with him. They knew how precious their time was because he would soon have to pack up and head out of town.

They took a trip to Disney world, lots of water parks where he loved watching Lina in the water. He was happy to hear that Valencia and Harley had been adamant that Lina learn how to swim early and at age two, she was swimming like a fish. They'd spent a lot of time with his parents where Lina would spend all of her time following behind her Poppy. He found it amazing to see his father light up every time Lina came through the door. Even today, Lina was playing between his father and Valencia's father who was also at the party. He and Valencia had mended their torn relationship and agreed to leave the past in the past as they all agreed to do. He was drug and alcohol free and loved being able to spend time with his children and grandchildren.

He and Valencia found time to go out on dates while either his parents or her sister watched Lina. It was during those times that they talked about their future and the love that was blossoming more and more each day. Strangely, they still avoided any talk about him leaving soon. Thoughts of that day would dampen their time together.

A highlight of his summer was the first night he and Reggie took their loves out on a double date. It was the first time Raina had seen Valencia since their high school days. Raina and Reggie were as close and she and Ethan had been and the four of them back together was the highlight of their evening. They talked about the old days. For the rest of the summer, Raina and Valencia had become inseparable, doing lots of things with the kids. Ethan looked on that as the way it was always meant to be. He watched as Lina ran around behind Reggie's oldest two children as if they had known each other for years. Lina may not be his biological daughter, but Ethan knew that she was the daughter he always wanted to have.

"Penny for all of your thoughts?" Moriah said walking up to the table where he stood watching the festivities.

"Oh, nothing really."

"It's more than nothing. I've been watching you as you watch Valencia and you look sad. I'm equating that to the fact that you're leaving soon. What are you thinking?" she asked.

Ethan turned around and faced her.

"I'm thinking I don't know how I'm going to leave Valencia and Lina here in Florida. I want them with me," he admitted.

"Then don't."

"Don't what?" he asked.

"Don't leave them here."

"I can't ask her to uproot her life again and move to Denver away from her family especially when I'll be on the road most of the time. Here, she at least has her family with her. She's just getting back together with them and look how happy they all are together."

"I know she's happy being back here in Florida, but the love the two of you share doesn't come around often. Very seldom does it come around twice. You won't know what she'd like to do until you talk about it. Have you talked at all about life after you return to Denver?" she asked.

"Not once. We've talked about the future and the fact that we plan to have a future together, but we have yet to deal with the fact that I'm returning home in two more days."

"Don't hide from the inevitable. I don't have to tell you what to do here because I think you know. As happy as you've been these past few weeks is the happiest I have ever seen you and I do mean ever. There is so much love between the two of you that I'm sure it can be seen from space. Don't let anything keep you from that."

Ethan smiled and gave her a hug.

"I hear you, Mom. I've been thinking about something and when a decision has been made, I'll call you immediately – how's that?"

"Sounds like my son is turning his first love into his happily ever after love."

"I'm trying. You have no idea how hard I'm trying."

Ethan turned to face the crowd and locked eyes with Valencia. He mouthed 'I love you' and she mouthed it back to him. He could see them in their future and it looked good. Whether she stayed in Florida or moved with him to Denver, they would always be together. If she wanted to stay in Florida, he would suggest that she and Lina move either into his condo or into the house. He knew she was thinking of finally moving out of Aimee's house and finding her own place. His homes were as much hers as they were his and he needed her to know that. He was ready to make their lives one. His prayer was that she was as ready as he was.

~~

After everyone had gone home for the night, Ethan put Lina to bed in the room they'd slimly decorated for her. He read her a bedtime story while Valencia enjoyed a candlelit soak in the hot tub in the master suite. He was about to begin a new book when he looked down and noticed Lina had fallen asleep. Tucking her in comfortably, he turned on the night light and left the bedroom door slightly ajar as he walked across the hall to the master suite just as Valencia exited the attached master bathroom with a towel wrapped around her body. He watched as she searched around in one of the dressers and pulled out a hot pink, silk night shirt. They had agreed to always sleep in clothing with Lina in the house.

"I take it she's asleep," she asked climbing into bed.

"She is and it only took one book tonight. With all of the people at the house tonight for your celebration, she wore herself out. Do you need me to read you a bedtime story to help you get to sleep?" he joked and joined her in bed after removing his top, but keeping on his pajama bottoms.

"Well, only if it's a good one."

"It's a really good one and I won't even need a book," he said turning on the light on the nightstand beside the bed. Pulling her into his arms as she laid her head on his chest he started his story.

"Well, my story starts with a man and a woman who spent many years apart and found each other again. Their love was as strong as ever, but there was one small detail about their love that they both avoided – what will happen to the new love they've built when he has to leave her and return to a life many miles away from her."

He felt Valencia perk up when she discovered he was talking about them.

"Oh, really?" she said joining in on the story.

"Yes, really. One day after having the perfect party at his house, she took a hot soak in the tub before joining him in bed where he presented her with an engagement ring, asking her to marry him and join him in life and love wherever life will take them. He promises to love her unconditionally for the rest of his life – he promises to love her daughter as if she were his and he hopes that she doesn't want to live apart from him anymore because they've spent enough time apart already."

When Valencia stiffened, he didn't know what to make of it when she didn't lift her head from his chest. Pulling a silver velvet ring box from under his pillow where he'd placed it as soon as he got into bed, he opened it right in front of her face and waited for her reaction.

As she slowly sat up and turned to him, tears that

had pooled in her eyes fell down her cheeks.

"Oh, Ethan! Are you sure? I know we haven't talked about what will happen in a few days when you return to Denver, but is this really what you want?" she asked.

"The question is what do you want? I love you and I want you to be my wife. If I've doubted anything in my life ever, this isn't one of those moments. I can't imagine going into this season with no permanency in our lives. I have contemplated this for a while now and when I talked to my mother earlier, she all but confirmed, without knowing what I had planned, that I have no intentions of leaving for Denver without you and Lina. I know it's a major decision you have to make because it would mean leaving your family to move to Denver where you won't know anyone."

"You want us in Denver with you?" she asked through tears.

"I want you and Lina wherever I am. If you want to stay here in Florida for the season, that's fine as long as I know you're my wife and where you are is where I will always be. I have the house and condo here, the house in Denver and another house in Los Angeles. I rarely spend time at my condo in New York, but pick any of those locations as our home base and that's where it will be. Any time you're feeling lonely, you can fly anyone into Denver or spend your time in Florida. Fly them to where you are – whatever will make you happy. All I want in life is to make you and Lina happy. I have always loved you and I always will. I want my first love to be my only love and my final love. There has never been anyone for me, but you. Will you marry me?" he asked again.

"Yes!" Valencia shouted and threw her arms around his neck and cried harder this time. Ethan held her until her weeping subsided.

"Thank you for coming back into my life," he said.

Valencia looked into his eyes, knowing she would always find love in them.

"Thank you for never forgetting the love we shared."

"You were my first love and my only love," he said.

"I love you," Valencia said as Ethan slid the large diamond down her finger and brought her ring finger to his lips for a kiss.

To top off their night, he turned on soft music and pushed the button to play the song he had already programmed to play or them tonight.

"I love you, too," he said.

As the sounds of Luther Vandross and Diana Ross singing, Endless Love, flooded the room, Ethan knew they really had come full circle. The moment she sang, 'my first love', he kissed Valencia reminding her that she was his first love.

With the ring on her finger and her love in his heart, Ethan rolled her under him, undressed her and spent the rest of the night showing her just how much he loves and cherishes his first love.

Enjoy this excerpt from an upcoming release from Cheryl Barton, *"Behind Closed Doors"* – Coming October 30, 2017

"So, do you know for a fact that Kennard is working today or was all of this scheming a waste of time?" Yasmine asked.

"Stop your worrying. You'll get to see your man today. I told you, the record company receptionist and I are tight and she would never tell anyone about you. Kennard's assistant will be leaving out and will be gone for about an hour and that means you have one hour. Kennard has to respect the level of risk you are willing to take to prove to him that you're interested in him. I planned this out perfectly if I must say so myself. I haven't worked for these slippery slope lawyers for the past year and not learn how to scheme and be conniving. Trust, I've helped sneak in enough side chicks for the married guys that I should go into business for this stuff," Aria laughed.

"Well, just make sure you keep dumb and dumber from finding out that I'm not in here with you."

"You know what, let me take care of that right now."

Yasmine watched Aria as she straightened her clothes and stood taller in her five-inch stilettos and pranced to her office door.

"Girl, I swear I'm correct. Let me ask your guys here who's right," Aria said loudly, putting on a show for the two bodyguards sitting in the waiting area. Yasmine knew it was all for show and a part of their plan to get her back out of the office unseen. She decided to play along to add more drama to the scene.

"I say I'm right, but feel free to ask someone else their opinion," she hollered.

"I'm telling you I'm right. Let me ask Lars and Roman." she said.

"Say guys, Princess Yasmine and I were having a discussion about penis sizes. I was telling her that I like them really long and very thick and that men know how important size is to a woman and we wanted to know what you thought? Are men as preoccupied with how big they are if they know women are all about the size?"

Yasmine had a look of horror on her face before she placed her hand over her mouth to stifle her laugh. Leave it to Aria, miss bold and beautiful, to not hold punches on a topic that she made men squirm. She was glad they were friends because she could live vicariously through her boisterous friend. Being a

Princess had its limitations, especially with the opposite sex. The fact that Aria could make such a statement with a straight face didn't surprise her. Nothing surprised her when it came to her best friend.

Yasmine watched as Lars and Roman turned as white as ghosts and looked to each other, not believing what they were just asked. They shouldn't be surprised since she relentlessly flirted with both of them every chance she got.

"What?" Lars said in response.

"Well, it's part of our lunch discussion and that's the tamest of the subjects. I figured, since we have the two of you sitting right out here, you can be our male perspective on everything. Trust me, the topics I have planned are going to blow you away. So, what do you say?"

Both men stood straight up out of their seats.

"Uh, we're going to take you up on that offer and hang out in the employee lounge. You said it was down the hall this way right?" Lars said, looking in any direction that wasn't at her.

"Are you sure? Well, if you really want to do that, yeah, it's at the end of the hall and cut a right. There's actually a nice lunch buffet in there today if you want to indulge. I know you feel like you can't let the Princess out of your sight, but I don't know how many questions I may need to ask you to break our tie in the discussions. I guess we'll have to figure it out for ourselves if you're going to the lounge."

"Yeah, why don't we do that because I'm starving.

What about you Roman?"

"Yeah, me too. Tell Yasmine, if she needs us, we're a few steps away and she has her panic button."

Aria faked a smile.

"Uh, huh. I'll let her know," she said and shut her office door back.

"You are out of your mind!" Yasmine shouted and jumped up and down with excitement. There was always such a rush being around Aria.

"I'm telling you, that performance was Oscar worthy. If nothing else, you know I can make a guy run away!" she shouted. "Now, let's get you upstairs to see your man. Did you bring condoms? If not, I keep a supply in my office drawer."

Yasmine snapped her head around so fast, she thought it would break off.

"Stop assuming I'll need a condom for anything. I simply wanted to see him and let him see that I'm not some stuck-up Princess, which is what he called me the last time I saw him. I like this guy and you know that and why do you keep a supply of condoms in your office? Just what do you do in here besides work? It's a law firm!"

"Oh, it's not for me. These attorneys may look like they're all work, but after hours and sometimes during the day, they get busy with all kinds of women and they can't be caught buying condoms since all but one of them is married. I get an extra added bonus by keeping them supplied with things like pens, paper, condoms and the morning after pill."

"What? You have the morning after pill in that drawer?" Yasmine asked, shocked.

"You don't want to know. Now, take a few of these condoms and get your pretty ass upstairs. You're wasting time with me when you could be getting busy with the sexiest man in LA."

Yasmine huffed at her.

"I told you, it's not about that."

"Well, it should be. It's been months since you've gotten laid and you're overdue, unless you've hooked up with someone since Vegas and that was six months ago, you're due. I can't have you walking around in heat all the time. Even a Princess needs to get her some and when I tell you there isn't a better specimen walking around then Kennard Jackson, I mean it. You've set your eyes on a beast of a man!"

Yasmine tried to look away to not give away the secret that she hadn't had sex in six-months which occurred on their girl's trip to Las Vegas.

"It doesn't matter because like I said, I just want to see him."

"Yasmine, no one just sees Kennard Jackson; they get a taste, a sample or a whole damn meal. If I were his type, I would have tried getting in those jeans a long time ago, but he likes his women, slim with big asses and large breasts and you fit that bill to a tee. Ugh, you frustrate me so. I have to teach you how to be a little more like me."

"Whatever."

"Okay, let's get you upstairs. There is an exit to the

fifteenth floor through the office over here. I'm going to call Cindy, the receptionist up there, to let her know to let you in. Those doors only open from that side. She'll get you to Kennard's office unnoticed and take as long as you need. I'm going to laugh ever so often just in case dumb or dumber comes by to check on us. Now, get going. When you're ready to come back down, she'll call me," Aria said pushing her towards the hallway that led to another door.

Yasmine bit her bottom lip, still unsure about what she was about to do. Throwing caution to the wind, she pushed the door open and rushed up the stairs.

Just as she reached the landing to the fifteenth floor, the door opened and a blond woman escorted her in.

"Hi, how are you? I'm Cindy and when you're ready to leave, have Kennard buzz me. I don't know how long his assistant will be, but if she comes back, I'll need to distract her to allow you time to get out unnoticed. Kennard's in his office which is the large set of doors at the end of the hallway. No one else is back there and I'll make sure no one comes back that way. He doesn't have a meeting for a few hours meaning you should be good to go," she said smiling.

Yasmine didn't respond, but shook her head signaling she understood as she walked quickly to the large set of dark redwood doors at the end of the hall. As she reached them, she looked back at Cindy who was still making sure no one saw her. She leaned toward the door and could hear Kennard talking on the phone. Taking in a deep breath, she knocked softly and waited for him to acknowledge that he heard it.

"Come in," he said.

"Here goes nothing," Yasmine said softly and opened the door.

She stood in the opened doorway until he looked up and saw her standing there. Whoever he had been talking to had completely lost his interest. For what seemed an eternity, they looked at each other as if they were strangers wondering what they were doing. To break the obvious trance, she smiled and waved a few fingers at him. When Kennard didn't move or respond, she didn't know what to do next.

Kennard had to blink several times to be sure the woman he saw standing in front of him was actually there.

"Yasmine?"

From the look of things, she was alone which surprised him since he never saw her without her security detail.

"I'm sorry if I'm disturbing you," she stuttered out.

"Disturbing me? Are you kidding? You're joking, right? You standing in my office looking like a dream? There is no such thing as you disturbing me.

"It looks like you're busy on a phone call," she said.

Kennard looked at the phone in his hand, forgetting he was having a conversation before she showed up.

"What this? Hey, Ben, I have to go. Let's continue this conversation a little later. I'll have my assistant ring you back later when I'm free because right now, anybody other than this gorgeous woman who is standing in front of me is obsolete."

Before his caller could respond, Kennard hung up and then reached for his phone again, tapping the intercom.

"Leslie, hold my calls and visitors, please."

Yasmine pointed to the outer office.

"Oh, she's not out there."

"She isn't? Then how did you get in here?" he asked inquisitively.

"Cindy."

"Remind me to make sure Cindy gets a raise. Now to what do I owe this surprised, but extremely welcomed visit?" Kennard asked.

The last thing he expected was to see Princess Yasmine standing in his office and to say she was gorgeous was again an understatement. She was even more beautiful than the last few times he'd seen her.

"Well, the last time we talked you called me a stuck-up princess and I wanted you to see that I'm not like that at all. I am a Princess, but I'm not stuck-up."

He eyed her from head to toe and his body hardened instantly.

Damn! He said inwardly. How could this woman do this to him every time? All he needs to do is look at her and his body reacts like some teenager.

Kennard stood from behind his black and gray marble-top desk, pushing his chair back as he walked around it to get closer to her. He smirked at his erection knowing that this was his state every time he set eyes on her. He purposely adjusted himself so that she could see him do it. He wanted her to know without a shadow of a doubt, that he wanted her, as much as he could read from her body language, that she wanted him.

He tried to reign in his desire for her and his boys reminded him that he was way out of his league with her, but he couldn't help himself. His eyes loved gazing upon her and his hands throbbed like his manhood at the thought of touching her. His lips wanted to devour hers with a powerful kiss and his tongue wanted to taste her until she screamed his name and only his name. He knew he should care more that she was engaged to marry another man, a man she herself had only met once in person, but he didn't care. The fact that she was here, in his office was enough for him to know that she didn't care about her impending marriage either. Right now, all he knew was that he was looking at her and she was real.

Finding words seemed impossible as silence ensued and neither said a word. Yasmine began to look uncomfortable and he liked that. He didn't want her comfortable; he wanted her aroused.

"Umm, maybe I should leave. I don't want to cause any trouble, especially for Aria, with my being gone."

"Aria is your friend, right? She works for the law firm a few floors down from here. What does she have to do with this?" he asked, curiously.

"She planned all this out for me to slip away from my detail in order to sneak up here to see you. We are supposed to be having lunch in her office and I have about an hour before Lars and Roman, my detail, will probably go in and check on me."

"Oh, then you have an hour, so don't rush off. You came to see me and I'm glad you did."

Kennard walked even closer to her as Yasmine backed up toward the door. Forgetting that she had closed it, she stopped when she encountered the door at her back.

"Ooops," she said, knocking into it.

"The door is closed," he said.

"So, did you come all the way up here just to see me or was there something else you wanted."

"I..I..I..don't know," Yasmine stammered.

"You don't?" he asked, sauntering up to her until he was only a breath away.

Yasmine wanted to look away from his piercing stare, but couldn't. Kennard was so damn sexy there was no way any woman would be able to take her eyes off of him. The way he was looking at her made her skin feel hot and moist and her thighs throbbed.

"Why are you so damn fine?" she asked, abruptly. She even caught herself by surprise by what she blurted out.

Kennard laughed and threw his head back.

"You know I get that a lot, but until this very moment, I never cared to pay much attention, but hearing it from you, I'm honored you notice and I'm thankful you said it. I never thought you'd be that bold. How bold can you be? I mean, I know how to make some pretty indecent overtures, but I don't want to scare you away."

"Am I sweating? I swear it's really hot in here?"

"Yes, you are and it's only hot right here in this space right around you and me."

Kennard reached out and placed his hand on the door right at the side of her head. When she turned to look at where he placed his hand, he leaned in and quickly kissed the side of her neck.

Now, he's done it, she thought. Not only were her thighs really throbbing, but now her sex was, too. His lips were soft and wet against her neck. Should she dare ask for more? Did she come for more? Was Aria right? Did she want Kennard to take her, like this in his office, behind closed doors? Hell, yes! Turning her head back to him, she held his stare and dared him to make another move.

"Like that?" he whispered close to her ear.

"Yes," Yasmine said softly.

Without thinking, she linked her finger in one of the hooks on his jeans and pulled him up against her and the moment she felt his erection, she knew what she came for. She should have taken Aria up on her office with the condoms.

"Oh, damn. I see you aren't stuck-up. You're a woman who knows what she wants. Well, you know what, I'm a man who knows what a woman wants and definitely what she needs and your need is written all over your beautiful face.

"I only have about forty-five more minutes?" she said, seductively.

Completely out of character, she wasn't holding back knowing she may never get an opportunity like this again.

"Sweetness, there is a lot that can be done in the forty-five minutes you have left, or should I say forty minutes because I want to be sure you have at least five minutes to make your escape back downstairs."

Yasmine looked at Kennard and to her he was a tiger that has set his eyes on his prey. His eyes seemed to darken as she began to feel his aura all around her.

With one hand on the door, Kennard used the other to use a finger and trace the small area where he'd placed a kiss. From there he used that same finger to travel down her neck until his finger rested in the middle of her large cleavage. He loved a woman with large breasts and Yasmine's were perfect. He watched her as she watched his finger and noticed her breathing had become erratic. That's exactly what he wanted. He wanted her to want him as bad as he wanted her.

"Forty minutes, huh?" she asked.

"Shall I show you what I can do in forty minutes behind closed doors?"

"Yes," she said without a hint of hesitation.

Kennard leaned into her neck and moved his mouth up to her ear.

"Turn around, place the palm of your hands against the door and hold on. It's going to be a bumpy, yet very enjoyable ride.

A Lovers' Heart Series

Book 1 – Heartthrob – Now Available

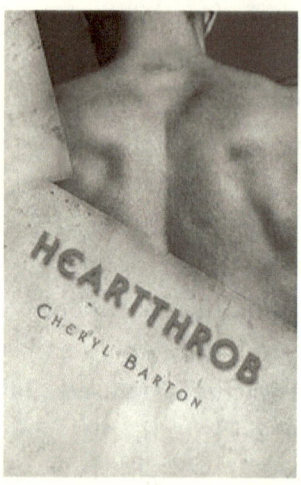

Cade Weston, Hollywood's most eligible bachelor and named the world's sexiest man of the year, lives life at the top with a bevy of beauties at his beck and call, people providing his every desire and more money than any one person should have.

Callie Hurston struggles to make it as a stylist to the stars in a world where women are intimidated by her beauty and men are interested in her body and not her talent.

Cade thought he had it all until he has a chance meeting with Callie and decides to take a chance on her talent and ends up taking an even bigger chance with his heart.

Can the playboy turn in his player's card and give in to love?

The Bachelor Series

Book 1 - Bachelor Not for Sale – Now available

Duron Knight agreed to take part in a bachelor auction held by his sister's sorority. Little did he know that he would find the woman of his dreams in the form of sexy bombshell Taija Charles, the woman in red.

Taija, in a room full of the sexiest men in Atlanta, has eyes for one handsome bachelor that no woman in her right mind could resist.

As sparks fly between them, can Duron put his unhappy past with women behind him and give his all to Taija? He may fight love, but Taija has plans to help him mend his broken heart with real love and a whole lot of lust.

Book 2 – A Designed Affair – Now available

In this follow-up to *"Bachelor Not for Sale"*, Loren Knight has been engaging in a secret love affair with her brother Duron's best friend and business partner, Michael Bailey. He is everything she could want and more in a man, but she believes the risk is too great for any type of relationship with him beyond their steamy encounters behind closed doors.

Michael Bailey has been fighting his attraction to Loren for years. He has stayed away from her out of respect for his best friend and business partner. Now that he and Loren have finally given into the passion they have been craving, can Michael convince Loren that what they share is worth the risk of even Duron finding out?

Book 3 – A Perfect Combination – Now available

In this second follow-up to *"Bachelor Not for Sale"*, Tyrone Davis is the king of one-night stands. The nickname, *Mr. Love'em* and *Leave'em*, given to him in his college days, still follows him as a top executive in the corporate world. He never believed in karma until it paid him a visit in the form of a very sexy and uninhibited one-night stand.

Victoria Alston couldn't forget the incredible night she spent with Tyrone Davis, someone connected to her best friends. In just one night, he stirred feelings in her she never thought she would ever experience. The next day, she disappeared, returning to reality and the fiancé she left back in Boston.

Tyrone and Victoria both soon discover that it wasn't just a one-night stand, but a perfect combination for the kind of love most people only dream about.

Book 4 – Love at Last – Now available

They had the perfect love...That's what Brian Knight thought of his relationship with Sherry Braxton until he looked up one day and she was gone and never wanted to see him again.

Two years later, he discovered that there is the possibility that Sherry may have been pregnant with his child. Hurt and angry at her deceit, he takes a flight to Baltimore to fight for his rights as a father and realizes that the love and passion they once shared had never died.

Is it possible he could still have the kind of love he thought would last a lifetime? Can he still have his love at last?

Upcoming new release - "On the Lam", book 1 of "The Game Changers" book series
Available September 30, 2017

Being rescued has never looked this sexy! If you have to be rescued, you want him to be a Navy SEAL and you want his name to be Dustin!

Other books by Cheryl Barton

Bachelor Series

Bachelor Not for Sale
A Designed Affair
A Perfect Combination
Love at Last
Twelve Bachelors for Sale – Coming Fall 2017

Amorous Occupations Series

The Artist
The Bookkeeper
The Chef
The Dancer
The Electrician

A Lovers' Heart

Heartthrob
Heartbeat – Coming September 2017

Inspirational Romance

Down, But Not Out: Breaking Chains

Stand Alone Romance

Holly for Christmas
Second Chances: Three Valentine Novellas
Un-Break My Heart
Bossy
Love on Top
Behind Closed Doors – Coming October 2017
Advantage, Love – Coming December 2017

Chapter 11

About the Author

Cheryl Barton lives in Maryland and in her spare time she loves to read espionage novels, cook, watch Sci-fi movies, spend time with family and friends and enjoy Maryland steamed crabs.

Indulge in more romance and inspirational novels by visiting her website at www.cherylbarton.net.

Cheryl is a member of the Black Writers' Guild of Maryland, Romance Writers of America – National Chapter and the Maryland Romance Writers.

Connect with me

Visit my website at www.CherylBarton.net
Twitter – @Author Cheryl Barton
Instagram – AuthorCherylBarton
Facebook at Author Cheryl Barton
Email – Cheryl@CherylBarton.net
Blog - https://mswriterinmd.wordpress.com/